A Troublesome Boy

For Lynda and Wayne.

A Troublesome Boy
Paul Vasey

Great meeting you on Pelee Island,

All the best

GROUNDWOOD BOOKS
HOUSE OF ANANSI PRESS
TORONTO BERKELEY

Paul
2012

Groundwood Books / House of Anansi Press
110 Spadina Avenue, Suite 801, Toronto, Ontario M5V 2K4
or c/o Publishers Group West
1700 Fourth Street, Berkeley, CA 94710

We acknowledge for their financial support of our publishing program the Canada Council for the Arts, the Government of Canada through the Canada Book Fund (CBF) and the Ontario Arts Council.

 **Canada Council   Conseil des Arts
for the Arts   du Canada**

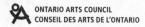 **ONTARIO ARTS COUNCIL
CONSEIL DES ARTS DE L'ONTARIO**

Library and Archives Canada Cataloguing in Publication
Vasey, Paul
    A troublesome boy / Paul Vasey.
ISBN 978-1-55498-154-0 (bound).—ISBN 978-1-55498-155-7 (pbk.)
    I. Title.
PS8593.A78T76 2012   jC813'.54   C2011-906231-3

Cover photograph by Josef Kubicek/Getty Images
Design by Michael Solomon

Groundwood Books is committed to protecting our natural environment. As part of our efforts, the interior of this book is printed on paper that contains 100% post-consumer recycled fibers, is acid-free and is processed chlorine-free.

Printed in Canada

For Marilyn

1

I WAS ALMOST fourteen and a half and already I was a failure. Capital A. Capital F. Don't take my word for it. Take the word of pasty-faced, pudgy-fingered, owl-eyed Gordon Little, head of guidance at Avery Bay Collegiate and Vocational Institute.

Words, actually, lots of them. Written in his old-lady fountain-pen handwriting on his pansy blue stationery and stapled to my report card so there'd be a telltale hole in the card if I ripped off the note and tossed it into the garbage where it obviously belonged.

Teddy is A Troublesome Boy. He is Disrespectful of his Teachers and Dismissive of his Classmates. He has A Major Problem with Persons in A Position of Authority. He is constantly challenging his Teachers and belittling the opinions of his Peers. Although he is undoubtedly An Intelligent Boy, he is A Failure when it comes to applying himself to his studies. As you can see, he has failed every course in Grade 9, with the exception of Art. We here at A.B.C.V.I. are at A Loss. Perhaps you are considering Another Course Of Action. Please Advise.

Henry, my mother's meathead move-in boyfriend, was not at a loss and he did have a course of action. He loaded me and my duffel bag onto a northbound Greyhound early one morning and shipped me off to St. Ignatius Academy for Boys. Thursday, August 27, 1959. You don't forget the day your life changed, that's for sure. St. Iggy's was part private school, part reform school. The perfect place for parents and the courts to unload their troublesome boys.

"Personally," said Henry, "I don't give a shit if you ever come back. But you won't be coming back until you get an A in every course you take. And until you lose that attitude of yours. Understood?"

I didn't answer him. I didn't have to. I let my eyes do the talking, gave him the big Fuck You Death Stare.

"Another thing." He was doing the pointy-finger thing with my chest. "You try running away from this place, I'll have your ass hauled into court so fast you won't know what hit you. I'll have you charged under the Juvenile Delinquent's Act and you'll wind up in the reformatory. That happens you won't see daylight for years. You have any idea how ugly it would be in the reformatory?"

Another poke in the chest. Another Fuck You Death Stare.

I turned my back, hoisted my duffel bag, got on the bus. If he was standing there watching as the bus pulled out I wouldn't know. I was slouched down, my knees pressed up against the seat in front of me, my Tigers hat pulled down over my eyes. But just in case he was still there watching to make sure I didn't make a leap for it at the last second, I held up my middle finger as we pulled away.

Attitude my ass.

Eight hours later, there I was in downtown Belleview. Population five thousand. Back of beyond. I was the only one who got off the bus and the driver wasted no time pulling out. Who could blame him? Belleview was a sorry-ass excuse for a town. They'd chopped down all the spruce trees and built the place on bald rock. Two blocks of two-story buildings on Main Street, faded signs, frayed flags, peeling paint. Four o'clock in the afternoon it looked like they'd already rolled up the sidewalks. A couple of rusted pickups, half a dozen old guys in denim coveralls and baseball caps waddling around. End of the world.

The bus stop was a diner. Linoleum floor, black and white squares, white walls. Counter on the right, ten chrome stools with torn leather seats. Six booths on the left, more torn leather seats. There were two pictures on the wall above the booths. One showed some snowy mountains. The other was of fishing boats in a harbor. The pictures were as faded as the rest of the place.

Back of the counter, one tired waitress. Black hair bunned up, cigarette hanging from the corner of her mouth, one eye squinted shut against the smoke trail. Bright red lipstick. Lots of it.

I took a stool.

"What'll you have, sunshine?"

"A one-way ticket out of here would do."

"Until that comes along?"

"Burger and fries. And a vanilla shake." I lit up an Export plain, waved out the match, dropped it in the ashtray. "Please."

Toothy smile.

"Goin' to St. Iggy's?"

I nodded. "How'd you guess?"

"You got that death-row look about you."

"Thanks."

"Good luck," she said. "You'll be needing it." She turned her back and hollered through the opening at the fat guy working the grill. A few strands of black hair were greased down on top of his head. "Burger and fries, Freddy."

"Way ahead of you, Rita. Burger's already on."

Rita worked up the shake. She put down a glass and the metal container, all frosty on the outside. Two straws in the glass. The shake was so thick it took me a second to get a good taste. Tasted like no shake I'd ever had.

"Good shake."

"My specialty."

Freddy wasn't as gifted. The burger was burnt, looked like a thumbprint in the bun, which wasn't all that fresh, and the fries were soggy. I finished them anyway. I was starved.

"Where you from?"

"Avery Bay."

"Where's that?"

"Down near Owen Sound."

"Geez," she said. "You're a long way from home. How come they shipped you off to St. Iggy's?"

"I'm a bad-ass little kid."

She laughed. "Mass murderer?"

"Failed grade nine."

"Well, maybe they can turn you into a mass murderer now that you're here." She laughed again. I liked her laugh. "How come you failed grade nine?"

"Screwin' around." I dropped my voice to do my best imitation of Henry. "Not taking advantage of my natural potential. Letting my gifts wither on the vine."

"Your father?"

"My mother's bonehead boyfriend." I lit up another smoke, waved out the match, stood up and extended my hand. "Teddy," I said. "Clemson."

Rita shook my hand. "Killer Clemson. Has a nice ring to it."

I sat back down, poured the rest of the shake from the metal container into the glass.

"Great shake, Rita. Think I'll have to come back for another one some time." I made a big sucking sound, moving the straw around at the bottom to get the last bit of shake.

I paid and left her a nice tip. Another toothy smile.

"Can you call me a cab?"

"Honey, I can call you all kinds of things. But cabs ain't one of them. No cabs in this town. Time for a hike. Hang a left out the front door, hang a right at the first street, put one foot in front of the other. You can't miss it. It's the big creepy place on the hill. Looks like a prison."

"Thanks."

"Good luck."

"You already said that."

"Where you're going, honey, you'll need a double dose of luck."

"Jeezus."

"What I hear, Jesus ain't been hangin' around St. Iggy's so much. You want my two cents' worth? Do whatever you need to do to keep yourself in the priests' good books. In their bad books you don't want to be."

———

ONCE YOU WERE off the main street you were in a wilderness of brick and frame bungalows, most of them needing paint. A couple of clunkers in most driveways. One on wheels, one on blocks — one for driving, one for parts. More junkers than Dandy Andy had in his wrecking yard back home. A few guys were sitting on the front steps in jeans and work boots, big guts hanging out the bottoms of their T-shirts, every one of them in need of a shave and a haircut. Most of them were drinking beer and smoking and swatting mosquitoes. Looked like they missed the last slow freight out of town and didn't have a clue what to do next.

A couple of blocks off Main Street and it was all uphill. I had to stop twice to catch my breath and switch my duffel bag from one side to the other.

Just when I was thinking St. Iggy's must be in the next county, there it was up at the top of the hill.

Rita was right. Jeezus creepy place. Red brick, three stories, rows of squinty windows. Looked exactly like a prison. All that was missing was the barbed wire, a couple of turrets and some beefy guys with big guns. There was a wide drive leading from the road to the double oak doors. The sign out at the road pointed up the driveway: ONE WAY.

Yank open the front door and the place had that school smell to it: heavy-duty industrial cleaner, like there was a bad stink they were trying to get rid of. There was a foyer just inside the door, terrazzo floor and pea-green walls, then eight steps leading up to the first floor. On the wall at the top of the stairs was a life-sized statue of Jesus nailed to the cross. Stab wounds, blood, bruises, thorns — the works.

Mom was right. "Catholics are a weird bunch." She was smoothing my hair and getting ready to say goodbye. "I only hope whatever they got isn't catching." I asked her what she meant. She mentioned something about praying to statues, lighting candles, worshipping over the bones of the dead. I had no clue what she was talking about. "You'll see," she said. Then she patted me on both cheeks, handed me my ball cap, pulled me close for a kiss, whispered "I'm sorry" in my ear. Henry was right behind me, rattling the keys to his Caddy.

Fucking Henry.

I climbed the stairs. Over the first door on the left was a sign that said OFFICE. No one in sight.

And then, right behind me: "Welcome, Mr. Clemson."

Jeezus. I just about jumped. I turned around and looked up. Big guy in a black robe, some kind of rope cinched around his waist. Wavy brown hair slicked back.

"We've been expecting you. I'm Father Stewart." He must have been six-four anyway. Built like a linebacker. "I'm the principal. Come into my office." He pushed through a swinging half-door and held it for me. "This way."

His office was as creepy as the rest of the place. Capital C. No windows, low light, bookshelves against two walls, no carpet, no pictures, a big wooden desk, wooden chair behind it, two wooden chairs facing it. A big crucifix on the wall behind the desk. More blood and thorns.

He looked at the crucifix, then at me.

"That's what we do with troublesome boys." Evil grin. "Just so you know."

"Thanks for the warning."

Stewart stood behind his desk. "Have a seat, Mr. Clemson."

I dropped my bag on the floor and sat. Stewart pulled a leather strap out of a pocket in his robe. Must have been a special pocket. The strap was a couple of feet long by three or four inches wide. He tossed it on the desk.

"Something else for troublesome boys."

You couldn't like a grin like that. He sat down, leaned back in his chair, put his hands together, touched the tips of his two forefingers to his lips like he was praying or something.

He looked at me for a moment. Then he sat up, picked his glasses up off the desk and put them on, picked up a bit of paper.

"Your reputation has preceded you, Mr. Clemson. I had a chat with your father this morning."

"He's not my father. He's my mother's live-in. And he's a dink."

Stewart looked at me for a few long seconds, then looked down at a piece of paper.

"He was good enough to read me Mr. Little's letter."

"What a surprise."

Another look. "I took some notes." Then he began reading. "'Teddy is a troublesome boy. He has a major problem with persons in a position of authority.' I could go on, but I think you're familiar with the rest of it." He took off his glasses and put them on the paper, leaned back in his chair and did the prayer thing with his hands again, gave me the stare. Then he sat up.

"Let's make a few things clear. First, you're not going to have a problem with people in a position of authority here, Mr. Clemson. You are going to be a model of respect for people in a position of authority. You are going to respect your teachers and your fellow students. You are going to be unfailingly polite. You are going to work hard and you are not going to fail any of the subjects you take. This is not a matter for discussion. I hope I'm making myself clear."

I gave him the stare.

"Am I, Mr. Clemson?"

"Are you what?"

"Making myself clear."

"I guess so."

"Let's try that again, Mr. Clemson. Am I making myself perfectly clear?"

"Yes."

"Yes, Father."

"Yes, Father."

"Good." He stood up, headed for the door. "Follow me."

We left his office, went through the outer office into the hall, past the creepy Jesus.

"I'm going to have Brother Wilbur take you to your dorm. But first I want to show you something."

At the far end of the hall, near the bottom of a set of stairs, he opened a door.

"Leave your bag on the floor and step inside, Mr. Clemson."

I dropped my bag and stepped into a cubicle the size of a broom closet. Same puke-green walls as the corridor, same terrazzo floor, single bulb in a wire-mesh cage on the ceiling. In the middle of the room there was a straight-back wooden chair, like the one in his office, facing the door.

"Have a seat, Mr. Clemson." I looked at him and then at the chair. I sat. "Now, I just want you to understand what I've been talking about. If we have any trouble with you, you'll find yourself in here. This is a time-out room. One of many, I should add. We won't have any problem finding one for you. Any time you step out of line, give anyone any lip, give anyone any trouble at all, you'll find yourself in a room like this and this is what that will feel like." He flicked off the light and shut the door.

Jeezus.

I just sat there for a moment, too startled to say anything or do anything. A minute. Two minutes.

I stood up and felt the door. No handle. Now what? I knocked on the door.

"All right," I said. "I get the message. You can let me out." Silence. I hit the door with the side of my fist. "Let me out of here!" Silence. "What the hell are you doing? Let me out of here." I banged on the door half a dozen times. Silence. I felt for the chair and sat down.

What in hell?

Ten minutes passed. Maybe fifteen. Then the door opened.

"I'm Brother Wilbur. Father Stewart asked me to show you to your dorm." Brother Wilbur was a scrawny little guy, wrinkled face, gray brush cut. He was wearing a robe, but a brown one.

"What the fuck was that all about?"

"Watch your tongue, my son."

"I'm not your son. And I want to know why he locked me in that fucking room."

"You'll have to ask him. And if you use that language once more, you'll be back in that room and this time it'll be for half an hour. Pick up your bag and follow me."

For an old guy, Wilbur was in pretty good shape. He was taking the stairs two at a time. Three flights of stairs. I was dragging my ass by the time I got to the top, and he was just standing there waiting for me. Wasn't even breathing hard.

"Seems you could use some time in the gym, Mr. Clemson. And you might want to think about quitting the cigarettes."

At the top of the stairs there was a landing. On either side of the landing were two stairs leading to double doors. He led me through the doors on the left. "This is the junior dorm." There were two rows of metal-frame single beds with gray blankets. He walked down the room and pointed to a bed, second from the end on the left.

"This is your bed. You'll make it every morning and it will look exactly like this. No wrinkles. You are issued two sheets, one pillow, one pillowcase, one blanket. Every Friday you'll change your sheets and pillowcase. One of the Brothers will bring a cart with fresh ones. You'll put the old sheets and pillowcase down the laundry chute over there." He pointed to a little rectangular door in the wall. "And those will be the only things you put down the laundry chute."

He gave me The Look, as though I was about to empty a wastebasket down there.

"The washrooms are through that doorway." He led

me to the far end of the room. White-tiled walls, white-tiled floor, gray marble partitions dividing the stalls. Urinals the size of little bathtubs.

There was a handyman working on one of the sinks. Big guy with a shiny face. It was the first thing you noticed about him. Kind of a choir-boy look, except he was maybe thirty-five or forty. About the same age as my dad. He had black curly hair that he combed straight back. Looked like he hadn't shaved in a day or so. He was a hefty guy. Not fat, just large. He was wearing a lumberjack shirt, blue jeans and cowboy boots. He smiled a lot.

Had the faucets off and was fiddling around with a wrench.

"How's it going, Mr. Rozell?"

The guy looked up. "Well, say." He seemed a little rattled. Wiped his hands on his jeans. "Pretty good. Except I had a little problem."

"What kind of problem was that?"

"I dropped one of the washers down the drain. Had to open up the drain to get it." He laughed. Nervous laugh. "Should have it done soon. All I got to figure out now is where all the pieces go."

Rozell looked normal enough, but sounded a bit dim. How tough was a faucet?

"Well, good luck with that."

"Thanks, Brother." Rozell went back to fiddling with the wrench.

Brother Wilbur led me back through the dorm. "Lights out every night at nine o'clock. Wake up at six o'clock."

"Six?"

"You'll have half an hour to dress and get to chapel."

"I'm not Catholic."

"All the more reason to get to chapel."

"Where do I put my stuff?"

"This way." He walked back the way we had come — down the steps, across the landing, up the other steps and through that set of doors. "This is the locker room. The showers are at the far end. You've been assigned locker 82."

"Where is everybody?"

"School doesn't start until Monday. Most of the boys will be arriving on the weekend. The ones who are here are down in the gym. Put your bag in your locker. I'll take you down."

I shoved my bag in the locker and shut the door.

"Your lock?"

"I don't have one."

"In that case, bring your bag with you. I wouldn't leave anything unlocked around here." We headed back down the stairs. This time Brother Wilbur took them on the run, and the gym was back down on the first floor. Christ.

I could hear the echo of voices before we got to the gym. Brother Wilbur opened the door. There were ten or eleven guys in there shooting hoops, screwing around.

Brother Wilbur checked his watch.

"It's seven thirty-five. You'll have twenty-five minutes. Then it's snack at eight, showers at eight-thirty. And as I mentioned, lights out at nine. Enjoy yourself, Mr. Clemson." He shut the door behind himself.

Cream-colored walls for a change. There were low wooden benches along both sides of the gym, but only one boy sitting. Scrawny little kid with spiky blond hair. Looked like he'd cut it himself, all tufts and divots. He was sitting there like a dink, reading a book. He had black-rimmed glasses and, when I got close enough to see, weird eyes. The most amazing blue I'd ever seen, but the eyes weren't lined up right. The right one looked directly at you but the left one looked over your shoulder, like he was watching someone creep up behind you.

I wasn't sure I wanted to sit beside him, but it seemed mean to sit on another bench since he looked so hopeless already.

I sat on the same bench, but at the far end. I dropped my duffel bag at my feet. He didn't say anything for a couple of minutes. He was watching the kids tossing the ball and chasing each other around the gym.

"Tim," he said finally. His voice was almost a whisper. I looked in his direction. "Cooper," he said. "Tim Cooper." He was looking at me with the one eye. "Hi."

"Teddy," I said. "Teddy Clemson."

"There's your coincidence of the day."

"What?"

"Our initials."

"Oh," I said. "Yeah."

"You new here?"

"Yeah."

"Me, too."

"What did you do to wind up in a place like this?"

"Break and enters," he said. "Seven of them."

"Seven?" You'd never guess it to look at him. Scrawny-ass little kid.

He was looking at the kids playing hoops. "Should've stopped after six, I guess." He turned to face me. Smirky little dimpled smile. "Live and learn. You?"

"Pissed off my mother's boyfriend."

"Boyfriends are such a pain in the ass," he said. He leaned to his right, pulled something out of his left pocket. "My mother had a whole string of them. One worse than the one before. Dunno how she developed such bad taste in men all of a sudden. My old man was all right, even if he did skip out on us. All these other guys were just assholes. Except the one who gave me this." He was holding a little bone-handled knife. Pushed a button and the blade flipped out. He smiled. "Looks like it might come in handy. Place like this." He pushed the blade against the bench, put the knife back in his pocket.

"Tell me about your life of crime."

He laughed. He slid down a little toward me. "It started out as a kind of joke. Some guys I knew bet I couldn't break into this place while the people were sleeping. One of my mother's boyfriends was good for something. The one who gave me the knife. Taught me how to pick locks and hot-wire cars. I was in and out of the first place in under five minutes, the woman's purse in my hand. Sixty bucks in cash in her wallet."

"How'd they catch you?"

"Worked the neighborhood once too often. The cops were waiting for me when I came out of the last place. The judge said I could take my pick: six months in juvenile or a year here. Hard to break out of juvie. I'll be out of here by the end of September."

"How?"

"Walk out the door. Head for the highway."

"You can take me with you."

"You're welcome to tag along. I'm going out to B.C. You can live on the beach year round out there. Just spend your time fishing and swimming, eating and drinking. Sitting around a campfire listening to the waves — '. . . and wreaths of smoke/Sent up, in silence, from among the trees!/ . . . . where by his fire/The Hermit sits alone.' Wordsworth." He held up *The Selected Poems of William Wordsworth*. From the looks of it — dog-eared cover, dirt smudges on the edges of the pages — he'd been reading the same book since he was six.

"You pansies just going to sit there or you gonna play?" The kid had black hair, major ducktail. He was about six-one, six-two. No shirt, all muscle, sweat and attitude. He was bouncing the basketball in front of us.

"Not interested," said Cooper.

"Yeah, I'm in." I turned to Cooper. "Watch my stuff?"

"Anything worth stealing in there?"

"Socks and underwear."

"I'll check it out." Same little smile.

It was quarter to eight. The jock's name was Billy Mather. He was in grade eleven. He was on the football team. He was also on the basketball team, as I found out when he started dribbling circles around me. I chased him up one side of the gym and down the other and never did get my hand on the ball.

I was winded ten minutes later when Brother Wilbur reappeared at the door and flicked the lights on and off.

"Let's go, gentlemen."

My bag was where I'd left it. Cooper had vanished.

I was bringing up the rear and Brother Wilbur was right behind me. At the end of the hall there was a cafeteria.

"Form a line," said Brother Wilbur. "Three cookies each. One glass of milk."

Against the far wall was a counter. At the far end there

was a tray piled with cookies, straight out of the box. Beside the cookie tray was another tray with plastic glasses and beside that was the milk dispenser. The Brother was a hawk, counting the cookies on each plate.

"Fifteen minutes, gentlemen." He consulted the clock on the wall.

"Are we allowed to talk?" This was the smart-ass who was walking with Mather at the head of the line.

"Don't try my patience, Mr. Grainger. It's been a long day."

Guys were choosing tables. Mather and Grainger were at one table with a couple of other guys. The rest were in twos and threes at tables nearby. I chose an empty table at the far side of the room. Brother Wilbur was hovering.

"Is there any place I can buy a lock for my locker?"

Icy stare. "Tuck shop is closed. You can try there tomorrow. Are you always anti-social, Mr. Clemson?"

"Usually."

"Anti-social boys are problematic. We do not like problematic boys here, Mr. Clemson. Join the boys at that table." He pointed at the table beside Mather's. I got up and shouldered my bag, took my plate and glass to the next table. Brother Wilbur was right on my heels.

There was Cooper, slouched in the doorway.

Brother Wilbur gave him the eye. "Who are you?"

"Cooper."

"Do you have a first name, Mr. Cooper?"

"Yeah. How'd you guess?"

Giggles and snorts from a couple of tables.

"Would you mind sharing it with us?"

"Tim."

"Where have you been, Mr. Cooper."

"Out having a smoke."

"Who gave you permission to go outside?"

"No one."

"You just walked outside by yourself?"

"Yup."

"Did you mean, Yes, Brother?"

"I guess."

"We don't do things around here without getting permission, Mr. Cooper. It's against the rules. And when you break the rules, as you have just done, you pay the price. Which in this case will be detention, Mr. Cooper."

"Detention? You shittin' me?" Sounded like someone choked on his cookie, spitting and coughing. "School hasn't even started. How can you give out detentions?"

"I can give out detentions whenever I feel like it, Mr. Cooper. And I feel like it right now. You'll report to the detention room tomorrow right after supper. Two hours. The first hour for disobeying the rules. The second hour for swearing."

Cooper made for the cookies.

"No cookies for you, Mr. Cooper. You're late and it's time to go up to your dormitory."

I pocketed my last cookie, put my plate and glass on the counter. We single-filed out of the cafeteria and up three flights of stairs to the dormitory. Cooper fell in beside me.

"Here," I said. I handed him the cookie.

"Thanks." Gone, in one bite.

"Locker room, gentlemen. Time for showers and bed."

"What's the routine?" This was a pudgy little kid, brush-cut brown hair, glasses, still sweating and flushed from running up and down the gym chasing Mather.

"The routine, Mr. Klemski?" said Brother Wilbur. "The routine is, you get out of your clothes and into the shower. Then you dry yourself off and get into your pajamas and get into bed. Can you handle that, Mr. Klemski?"

Klemski nodded.

"Well, then, get moving."

Klemski and the rest of us got out of our clothes and walked naked down the locker room and into the shower room. Brother Wilbur stood in the doorway. Across from him was a table piled with towels. You had to inch between Wilbur and the table to get into the showers. The shower room was long and narrow, white tiles on the floor and the walls.

"Let's get to it, gentlemen."

A priest showed up in the doorway. Black hair. Big shoulders. Big hands.

"I'll take over here, Brother."

You could tell Brother Wilbur wasn't expecting this. He had a kind of what-the-hell look on his face, like he'd just been outranked.

"Yes, Father Prince. Of course." Wilbur made himself scarce. Father Prince took over in the doorway. "Let's go, gentlemen. We don't have all night."

We were all sizes, all shapes: thin kids and tubby ones, scrawny ones and muscled ones. And what seemed to matter most to Father Prince came in every size and shape as well: stubby ones and dangly ones, short and long, circumcised and not.

We soaped and scrubbed. He watched. It gave me the creeps. Capital C.

"That'll do, gentlemen. Turn off the water."

One by one we shut the water, grabbed a towel and started heading for our lockers.

"Towel off here," said Father Prince. "Drop your towels in the hamper, then go to your lockers and get your pajamas."

He watched us the whole while.

I pulled my bag from my locker, unzipped it. Right on top, a note from Cooper. *You're right. Nothing worth stealing. But you shouldn't trust anyone in a place like this.*

I looked across the aisle. Cooper had the last locker on the far side of the row. He was pulling on his pajama bottoms. I held up the note. He smiled. I got into my pajamas and shoved the duffel bag back into the locker, hoped Cooper was right about nothing worth stealing.

"Let's go, gentlemen."

We single-filed out of the locker room, down the steps, across the landing, into the dormitory and into our beds. Father Prince switched off the lights. The door clicked shut behind him.

A couple of minutes later, from one of the beds near the door: "No jerkin' off, boys." Laughter. Someone was bouncing on his bed, making the springs squeak. More laughter. Then the place quieted down. A little later someone was snoring.

I lay on my back, staring at the ceiling that was bathed in a red glow from the exit sign over the door at the end of the dorm.

My mind was buzzing. Bad thoughts. I could have killed Henry. I should have killed him the first night he slept over at our house. Smug bastard. The look on his face when it became obvious he was there for the night, that he was going to be pulling back the covers on my father's side of the bed and getting in beside my mother. A kind of so-what-are-you-going-to-do-about-it smirk on his fat face.

What the hell was my mother thinking, shacking up with a car-salesman goof like him? What the hell was my father thinking, walking out on us in the first place so he could go screw his secretary, leaving the door open so a snake like Henry could slither right in?

Thanks, Mom. Thanks, Dad.

I could have killed both of them.

Thanks to them, here I was in some weird school where sicko priests locked people in closets just because they felt like it, told you where to go and how fast.

I had a bad feeling. I was with Cooper. There was no way I was going to last a year. If he was out, I was out with him. B.C. sounded pretty good to me.

I was drifting off, visions of beaches and ocean in my head, when the door opened. I turned to look: the silhouette of a priest, rubber soles squeaking on the floor as he made his way down the aisle between the beds, flashlight in hand. He paused at the foot of every bed, shining the light on the sleeping faces. He stopped at the foot of Cooper's bed just across from mine, two down.

It was Prince.

He ran the light slowly from Cooper's feet to his face, then back down to his feet, then back up to Cooper's crotch. He stood there for a moment, just looking down at Cooper, then flicked off the flashlight, turned and walked back down the dorm and out the door.

Jeezus.

2

BY THE SECOND week of September, Cooper had become a kind of hero. He was famous for turning up, hair a mess, shirt-tail hanging out, dragging his ass into class a few minutes after the rest of us had settled into our seats, reciting poetry in the hallways and in the yard and even in the john, staying by himself — one of the "*vagrant dwellers in the houseless woods*" — as much as it was possible to stay by yourself in St. Iggy's. He became a pro at getting detentions.

"Mr. Cooper?"

"Yeah?"

"Did you mean to say, Yes, Father?"

"No."

"Try saying, Yes, Father."

Cooper would purse his lips, cross his arms over his chest, slide down in his seat, and the priest would scribble another detention slip to be presented at the door of the detention room, the slip outlining the offense (Insolence, Repeat Offense) and the punishment (Two Hours).

Cooper became the Whiz of Awkward Questions.

Father Bartlett taught religious studies. The Pear, to us. He looked like one. Small little head, hardly any shoulders, mile-wide ass.

One day he was going on about the Jesuits in Upper Canada. He was in his element. Once he got to Brébeuf and Lallemant he was beside himself. He sang the praises of the selfless priests whose only goal was to help the natives and pave the way straight to heaven. The Indians, of course, saw things differently, tied them to stakes, scalped them, poured boiling water over them, sliced up their bodies.

"The brave Brébeuf did not utter a single cry. In fact, he was so brave that after he finally expired the Indians cut out his heart and ate it, hoping that by doing so they might become as brave as this saintly priest."

Cooper's hand shot up.

"Yes, Mr. Cooper?"

"How do you know that?"

"Know what?"

"That he died without uttering a sound."

"It's been written by the historians."

"How did they know?"

"There would have been witnesses."

"Indians?"

"I would suppose so."

"And who would they have told their stories to?"

"To whom would they have told their stories?"

"Yeah. To whom."

"Other priests."

"My point, exactly."

"What point is that?"

"The priests would obviously want to paint themselves in the best light. Better a brave Brébeuf dying without a sound than Brébeuf all snotty and crapping himself and begging for his life. What else would the priests write down? It's all just a bunch of church propaganda. It's all bull."

"That'll be enough, Mr. Cooper."

It was never enough for Cooper.

"Another thing," he said. "What is it with you guys and bones?"

"What bones?"

"Brébeuf's bones. The priests who came to get his body boiled him. Boiled him, for God's sake!"

"Careful, Cooper." The Pear gave him the Big Furrowed Brow.

"Kept his skull and bones," said Cooper. "Put them on display somewhere and now people pray over them. If the Indians did that you'd call them savages."

That was it for Cooper. Again.

"Step outside, Mr. Cooper." Cooper stood up, collected his books and followed The Pear out the door. Whistles and applause. Then we heard the door of the time-out room close. And then, kind of echoey, Cooper's voice.

"You want to check your brains at the door, be my guest. But don't expect me to buy that bullshit."

No one saw Cooper again until supper time.

He was a regular in the time-out room. Two or three times a week. Sometimes for an hour, sometimes for an entire morning. One week, Father Dyer locked him up in the middle of the last period in the afternoon — "What kind of nitwit could possibly believe that Mary was a virgin?" — and left him there until lights out, when Father Dunlop looked around the dorm and wondered, "Where's Cooper?" Cooper came out grinning, and he was even grinning when Dunlop made him go back and mop up the puddle of piss he'd left behind.

Cooper and me were hanging around just about every day. Laughed and joked, went out and had smokes together. Talked a blue streak.

One afternoon we were sitting on a bench out in the yard.

"What do you want to do, Teddy?"

"Do?"

"With your life."

"Paint and draw," I said.

"Be an artist?"

"I guess."

"How come?"

"It's the only thing I'm any good at."

"What kinds of things do you draw?"

"Boats, cars, houses, beaches, farm fields. Whatever catches my eye."

"People?"

"Sure."

"Me?"

"I've already done you. Maybe a dozen times."

"You shittin' me?"

I opened up one of my notebooks, flipped the pages until I found a sketch of Cooper that I'd done in the margin.

"Here." I turned the book so he could see himself.

"Not bad," he said. "Even looks a little like me."

"Fuck off." I flipped through the notebook, found a few other sketches of him — some in profile, some full face, one showing just his eyes.

"I always thought I was kind of weird looking. On account of my eyes."

"You're not weird looking, Cooper."

"Do you think I'm good looking?"

"You're not the ugliest kid at St. Iggy's."

He smirked, reached over and gave me a shove. Almost sent me off the end of the bench.

Squirrely eyes or not, Cooper was becoming everybody's favorite at St. Iggy's. Even Mather and Grainger and the other jocks who thought at first he was some kind of poetry-reading pansy dink now thought he was about the coolest thing since sliced bread. Anyone tried to mess with him, Mather and his jocks would move right in and defend him.

Anyone except the priests. There wasn't much anyone could do about them, and they had it in for Cooper. Capital I.F.C.

Cooper almost seemed to like it. "You got a bull's-eye on your back, wear it proudly." He was always the last kid in dorm to haul his scrawny ass out of bed in the morning. When the priest of the day flicked the lights on sharp at six and hollered, "Rise and shine, ladies," most of the kids jumped right out of bed. A few would moan and groan and complain but then they'd get up, too, doing their best to hide their early-morning boners behind crossed hands.

And then there was just one lump left in one bed.

"Mr. Cooper, would you care to join us for our morning routines?" A grunt. Sometimes a fuck off if he felt like spending the morning in The Dungeon.

Most mornings, though, he would haul the covers up over his head and wait until the priest came along and gave him a sharp rap on the crotch with his yardstick.

"Haul it, Cooper. Now!" Cooper would get up as slowly as it was possible to get up, giving the priest in charge the evil eye.

"Beds, gentlemen. You, too, Cooper."

We had to make our beds military style: plump up the pillow, tuck in the sheets and blankets so there were two neat diagonal creases at either side of the foot of the bed. If there was a wrinkle anywhere on the blanket, the priest would rip the blanket and sheets right off the mattress and dump them on the floor. "Let's give that another try."

Once the last of the beds had passed inspection, we had fifteen minutes to go to the john, throw some water on our faces, comb our hair and climb into our clothes. Six-thirty we were out the door and heading down the stairs.

"Come along, gentlemen. You, too, Cooper. Time to have a word with The Lord."

"I'm not feeling particularly conversational this morning, padre."

"Be that as it may, Mr. Cooper, the Lord may wish to have a word or two with you."

"He hasn't felt the need so far. And I'm going on fifteen."

"Patience in all matters, Mr. Cooper. Patience in all matters."

Chapel was agony. We were all sleepy and hungry and pretty well everyone was dying for a smoke (except the few of us who had made it a habit to get up early and slide into the john, where we cracked open the window and lit up).

"I'm not even Catholic," I said. "How come I have to go to chapel every morning?"

"We're hoping for miracles, Mr. Clemson. Hoping for miracles. We are praying constantly."

"Patience in all matters, Father. Patience in all matters."

———

THE CHAPEL WAS at the back of the building. There were double oak doors and just inside them a little pot of water that the Catholics dipped their fingers in, making a sign of the cross over themselves. One of many weird things the Catholics did.

The pagans sat at the back, in the pew just inside the door. There were eight of us, including me and Cooper. We got our own personal Brother.

Brothers were sort of like priests, but a notch down. They had brown robes and they didn't get to do the big jobs like working the altar. They were sort of helpers, doing odd jobs like guarding the pagans during chapel. Brother Joe usually got the nod.

I liked Bro Joe. He was probably forty-five or fifty, gray wavy hair and gray beard. A bit simple, but nice. When he wasn't guarding us his main job seemed to be to tend the gardens around the building and feed the birds. All summer and fall he slept out under the trees in a sleeping bag. Someone said he actually slept out there in the winter sometimes. In the morning he'd just be a lump under a drift of snow. Weird, but nice.

Bro Joe never ragged us out like the priests did. If we got a little noisy, started giving each other the elbow, stuff like that, he would just lean forward and look down the row of us and raise a finger to his lips. We didn't like to hassle Joe, so we pretty much behaved.

The Catholics were herded right up front where the priests could keep an eye on them. Chapel was incense and hocus-pocus, all in Latin. I didn't have a clue what any of it meant. I just closed my eyes and went along for the ride.

The Catholics were a lot more trouble than we were, forever smacking each other in the crotch and giving each other the wet finger in the ear, ripping big wet farts. There was hardly ever a chapel service where one of the guard priests wasn't hauling a Catholic out of the pews by the ear and dragging him out the door and into the hall. You could hear the whacks and slaps and the kid hollering out in pain. Then a minute later the kid would come back in all hunched over and red-faced, the guard priest right behind him, shoving him on the back and giving all the other kids one of those you-could-be-next looks.

So far this morning, no serious crimes up in the Catholic section. At the back, we were all pretty much semi-conscious.

The priest in charge was droning along. *"Pater noster, qui es in ..."*

I nudged Bro Joe. "What's he saying?"

"The Our Father," said Joe. "You know, 'Our Father who art in Heaven.' You do know that, don't you?" He gave me a kind of sad little look.

"Oh, yeah," I said. "I know that one. Backwards and forwards."

Joe leaned toward me, all whispery. "Did you ever go to church? Before you came here, I mean."

"Oh, yeah." I didn't want to hurt his feelings. Truth was I hadn't been in a church in years before I turned up at St. Iggy's.

Joe gave me a little nudge with his elbow. "Here's one for you."

The priest up front was really getting into it, his voice echoing around the walls and up to the rafters: *"Domine Iesu, dimitte nobis debita nostra ..."*

"What's that mean?"

"Oh, my Jesus, forgive us our sins, save us from the fires of hell: lead all souls to heaven, especially those who are most in need of your mercy." Joe gave me a special nudge right there.

"Oh, my Jesus," whispered Cooper. "Save us from babbling priests. Lead us into the cafeteria so we can get some fucking breakfast."

Father Sullivan came charging down the aisle, gave Bro Joe a death stare for letting things get out of hand in the pagans' pew, grabbed Cooper by the ear and hauled him up to his feet.

"Jesus, man, you're going to rip my fucking ear off."

Sullivan's eyes lit right up. I half expected flames to shoot out. He gave Cooper a whack on the side of the head that sent him reeling, then picked him up off the floor and hustled him out the door.

Holy shit. My heart was racing.

"You're going to pay for this outrage, Cooper. You're going to pay dearly." The doors swung shut.

If Cooper had been cool for another five minutes, he'd have been wolfing down cold scrambled eggs and greasy sausages with the rest of us.

There were four long rows of wooden tables in the cafeteria, wooden chairs on either side, the kind that could be folded up and stacked. On the counter along the one wall were boxes of cereal, stacks of cold toast, jam and peanut butter. A little further on were vats of porridge like gray barf, lumpy and disgusting. Further on, powdered scrambled eggs, warm if you were lucky, but tasteless; sausages that made a pool of grease on your plate and were pretty well always cold.

"What do they do?" Anderson wondered. "Cook all this stuff in the middle of the night and just leave it out?"

I took some eggs and sausage, two slices of toast with

peanut butter and jam, headed to our table by the door. We left an empty chair in Cooper's honor. Hatfield put half a piece of toast, minus one bite, on the table.

"A burnt offering for Brother Cooper." We all laughed.

"One of these days one of these priests is going to kill Cooper," said Klemski.

"Nah," said Anderson. "They can't kill him. It'd be against their religion."

"Against their religion?" said Klemski. "You haven't been reading your history, Anderson. The Catholics are about the most bloodthirsty cult in the history of the world. They've started more wars than the rest of religions combined. Ever heard of the Spanish Inquisition? My God, Catholics have killed millions down through the years. What's one more sniveling little heretic?"

Klemski reached over and picked up the piece of toast that Hatfield had left in Cooper's place.

"He won't be needing this," said Klemski. "Besides, wasting food is a sin." He took a bite. "What I don't get is all this love-thy-neighbor and turn-the-other-cheek crap. If they really believed any of that, they wouldn't be beating the shit out of Cooper."

"You got a point there," said Anderson, mouth full of toast.

"You are disgusting," said Hatfield. "No one ever teach you not to talk with your mouth full?"

Anderson laughed, and then coughed. Toast flew everywhere.

"Jesus," said Hatfield, wiping toast bits off his shirt. "That is so gross."

"Hatfield! I heard that," said Brother Wilbur. "Step over here."

When he came back, Hatfield had a detention slip: Blasphemy. Two hours today, two hours tomorrow. Brother Wilbur had underlined Blasphemy.

"Shit," Hatfield whispered. "Today is football practice."

"Mr. Hatfield! Would you mind joining me here for a moment?"

When he came back he had another detention order. Swearing. One hour.

"How did he hear that?" whispered Anderson.

"I can hear through walls, Mr. Anderson. And I can see around corners and I can read minds and I can see in the dark. Something you should all remember."

The rest of breakfast was pretty quiet. A couple of mushrooms of conversation, the odd dropped knife or fork and a couple of farts. Hatfield came out with one of his terrible jokes.

"What do you call a dog with no back legs and steel balls?"

"I give up," said Anderson.

"Sparky."

Groans all around.

Anderson was turning his scrambled eggs over with his fork. The eggs had congealed into one big mass.

"Eggs shouldn't behave like this."

"The cooks are all retards," said Campbell. Campbell's hair was so red and wild it looked like his head was on fire. "That's the only problem with the eggs."

"It's not just that," said Anderson. "Don't you taste something weird? There's some kind of metallic taste. Not just in the eggs. It's in the sausage, it's in everything."

"What?" said Hatfield. "You think they're trying to poison us?"

"Not exactly," said Anderson.

"Then what, exactly?"

"I dunno. Something to mess with the way we think."

"C'mon," said Hatfield. "You don't really believe that, do you?"

"I wouldn't put anything past these bastards."

"Mr. Anderson!"

Swearing. One hour. That pretty well shut up our end of the cafeteria. We finished our breakfast, except for Campbell who said now everything tasted metallic and he wasn't going to eat again all day.

"Time's up! Trays to the window."

I wrapped up my toast in a paper napkin, opened a button, shoved it inside my shirt.

"Saving for a rainy day?" said Klemski.

"Something like that."

After breakfast we had clean-up. Brush your teeth, comb your hair, make yourself presentable if possible. Then we had half an hour before classes. Some guys finished their homework. Most of us headed outside. Klemski turned toward the stairs leading up to the dorm. I turned the other way.

"Where you going?" said Klemski.

I patted my shirt. "Got a little errand."

"Jeezus," whispered Klemski. "They catch you, you're dead."

I took the back stairs to the second floor. There were two time-out rooms by the chapel, one on either side of the hall. I opened the door on the right. Then I opened the one on the left. Cooper looked up, startled. His face was all red from where Sullivan had shoved him against the pew.

"You all right?"

"Yeah."

I opened my shirt, pulled out the toast, tossed it to him.

"See you later." I shut the door, flipped on the light and made for the stairs to the dorm. A little echoey "Thanks" from Cooper.

Five minutes later, Klemski and I were standing in a little alcove outside the back door.

The playing fields — football, track, baseball diamond — were out back, the whole area fenced off, fences lined with the spruce trees where Bro Joe liked to roll out his sleeping bag. It actually looked kind of nice out there and you could imagine for a little while that you were somewhere else, somewhere more or less normal.

A bunch of guys were playing pickup soccer, whooping and hollering and elbowing each other to the ground.

"Heathens." Klemski definitely could not do sports. He was a pork chop, five feet nothing, had to be close to 180 pounds. One flight of stairs would leave him all sweaty and out of breath. Fat, out of shape, but smart. I loved to get him going.

"What exactly is dogma, Klemski?"

"Dogma is what comes out of your mouth once you've shut off your brain." Then he was on about priests.

"They've been brainwashed since they've been in diapers. Priests filled their heads with horror stories from the time they were old enough to walk. 'Do this and you'll go straight to hell. Do this and you'll go straight to heaven.' Now they're doing the same. Organized religion is all about controlling people, making them do what you want. Scare them witless and you have them eating right out of your hand and filling up the collection plate every Sunday. They don't call their followers sheep for nothing, Clemson. That's why they're so keen to get you and me and the rest of the heathens to go to chapel. I don't think they should be able to force us to listen to that crap."

"What are you going to do about it?"

"I've written my cousin. He's a lawyer. I asked him to threaten to sue the bastards unless they stop forcing their religion down our throats. I'm expecting his reply any time now." Klemski had the most amazing grin. Somewhere between smugness and absolute evil. "If you want people to listen to you, you have to speak a language they can understand. Say this about the priests, they certainly seem to understand when you start talking money."

Then the bell rang.

Classes began at eight o'clock sharp. Four classes in the morning — geography, math, history and English. An hour for lunch and then four more in the afternoon — religious studies, art, gym and science. It was enough to fry your brain.

Geography, math and history passed without incident. No detentions. No one sent off to The Dungeon.

It was too good to last. In English we were studying *Oliver Twist.* Last period before lunch, our stomachs growling.

"Dickens makes great use of symbolism in all his novels and *Oliver Twist* is no exception," said Father Sullivan. "So perhaps that would be something worth discussing." Sullivan was tall, white-haired and hefty. Looked like he might weigh about two-twenty. Would've made a good truck driver, or a deckhand.

He was walking with his hands behind his back, but now he stopped at the front of the class and he was giving us the beady eye, searching for a victim.

"Mr. Cruickshank."

"Yes," said Cruickshank.

"Yes, Father," said Sullivan.

"Yes, Father."

"Let's try that again, standing up, if that wouldn't be too great an inconvenience."

Klemski and I shot each other glances. This was not going to end well. Looked like Sullivan still had a burr up his ass from chapel.

Cruickshank stood six-two and couldn't have weighed more than a hundred and twenty pounds. He was so skinny it looked like his pants would drop right off him. His face was constantly erupting and he couldn't resist the urge to pick and scratch. He looked like he'd just escaped from the contagion clinic.

"Now, then, Mr. Cruickshank. Have you been reading *Oliver Twist?*"

"Yes, Father."

"Very good, Mr. Cruickshank. Have you been enjoying it?"

"Yes, Father."

"Which parts have you particularly enjoyed?"

"The bits where the kids run around stealing."

"And why do you like those 'bits,' as you so quaintly call them?"

"The kids are cool."

"Cool?"

"Yes, Father."

"Thieving little scoundrels are cool, are they?"

"I think so."

"And why is that?"

"Because they've had a miserable life."

Sullivan was on the prowl again. "They've had a miserable life and have turned now to a life of crime." Sullivan was nose to nose with poor Cruickshank. "And for that, for turning to a sordid life of crime, they are rewarded by Mr. Cruickshank with the description of being 'cool.' Is that correct, Mr. Cruickshank?"

Cruickshank was sweating and his zits were flaming.

"Yes, Father."

"Tell me something, Mr. Cruickshank. Is stealing good or evil?"

"Evil, I guess."

"You guess."

"Yes, Father."

"Well, then, if stealing is evil, what does that tell us about the thieves?"

"That depends," said Cruickshank.

Klemski and I looked at each other. Klemski's eyebrows shot up.

"Depends on what, Mr. Cruickshank?"

"If they're poor and have no other way to feed themselves or take care of themselves."

"So what you are positing here, I take it, Mr. Cruickshank, is a world of conditional morality. Is that correct?"

"I guess so."

"In your world, if someone is poor, is it permissible for that person to steal?"

"If they're starving and no one is helping them, then yes."

"So would the starving thief be good or evil?"

"I'm not sure he'd be either good or evil."

"What *would* he be, pray tell?"

"Just a thief," said Cruickshank.

"But isn't thieving, in and of itself, an evil activity?"

"Not necessarily."

"Not necessarily?"

"I don't think you can just divide the world up into good and evil," said Cruickshank. "I think that's pretty simple."

"You think good versus evil is simple?"

"Yes."

"Do you think the Bible is simple, Mr. Cruickshank?"

"I don't know."

"Well, the Bible is all about good versus evil. So would that make it simple?"

"I guess."

"And if I see the world as a battleground for the forces of good versus the forces of evil, would that make me simple, Mr. Cruickshank?"

"I guess."

Sullivan grabbed Cruickshank by the front of his shirt and danced him backwards down the aisle until he had him against the back wall. Every head in the room was cranked around to see what would happen next.

"Are you calling me simple, Mr. Cruickshank?"

"I guess so."

"Are you calling my religion and my faith simple?"

"I guess so," said Cruickshank.

Holy shit.

Sullivan lifted Cruickshank right off the floor and slammed him against the wall. Cruickshank's back hit the wall first, and then his head bounced off it. Sickening sound. Sullivan slammed him against the wall again. Another sickening thunk. This time Cruickshank's eyes rolled back into his head. His face got all chalky. Sullivan let him go. He fell to the floor. He was twitching and coughing. It was the only sound in the room.

Sullivan left him there.

"When you gather yourself together, Mr. Cruickshank, you can make your way to the time-out room. Close the door behind yourself. Spend your afternoon thinking about the ramifications of mocking another man's faith."

———

"Sullivan is one sadistic sonofabitch," said Klemski.

We were huddled together at one end of the pagans' table. Anderson was inspecting his sandwich, lifting the top piece of bread and moving the filling around with his finger, like he was expecting maggots to crawl out.

"I'm not sure what they put in this sandwich," he said. "But it doesn't taste like tuna."

"That's because it's turkey, you moron." Klemski shook his head.

"That sonofabitch is going to kill someone," said Henderson.

"Look what he did to Cooper," said Anderson.

"Look what he did last week to that poor bastard in grade twelve," said Henderson.

Guy named Morris had lipped off to Sullivan. Some smartass comment. Sullivan told him to stand facing the wall. Left him there for a few minutes, staring at the paint, then came up behind him and slammed his face into the wall. Broke the poor bastard's nose. Blood everywhere. He was still walking around with a bandage over his nose.

We took our trays back to the kitchen window, unloaded the plates and glasses.

Anderson, Henderson and Klemski headed for the yard.

"I'll catch you in a few minutes," I said.

"Going to jerk off?" said Klemski.

"Yeah. Shouldn't take more than forty seconds," I said. They were all laughing as they headed down the stairs toward the rear doors.

I waited until they'd gone out. Then I went down to the basement and the boiler room.

I'd come across it by accident one day after supper. It was pouring like crazy and I didn't feel like getting soaked to the ass trying to have a smoke. So I went down to the basement and wandered around looking for a quiet place where I could light up and not have to see anyone or talk to anyone. It had been one of those days when I couldn't take another ten minutes of hanging around with anyone. I tried a few doors until I came to one that wasn't locked. Great room full of boilers and pipes, warm and dry, not a soul in sight. I spent half an hour in there, then picked up my butts and headed back upstairs. Since then, I'd gone down to the boiler room a couple of times.

I opened the door, did a quick scan of the room, then shut the door behind myself. I headed for the back corner where I could open a window and let the smoke out.

"Back again, eh?"

Jeezus. I just about jumped.

It was the faucet guy.

"You keep comin' down here, I'll have to put you to work. I'm Rozey," he said. "Roh-zhay Roh-zell. The handyman."

I reached out a hand. "Nice to meet you. I'm Clemson. Teddy."

Rozey was sitting on an old chrome-legged chair right under the window. Same shiny face. Same lumberjack shirt and blue jeans. Still smiling.

"Pull up a box," he said. "Take a load off." There were a couple of wooden boxes over near the wall. One was full of tools and crap. The other was empty. I picked it up and took it over near where he was sitting, set it on its end and sat down.

I pulled out my smokes. "Mind if I smoke?"

"Not if you're sharing." He smiled. I offered him one. He pulled out a Zippo lighter. There was an engraving of a cowboy on the front.

"You've seen me down here before?"

"Sure. Three or four times. You always take your butts with you. I like that."

"What do you do around here?"

"I'm the janitor. I clean up, mostly. That's the main thing. Sometimes I fix things. Try to. Taps, toilets, broken windows. Stuff like that."

"Did you come here to go to school?"

"No. I went to the town school. I didn't do so good. I

only got my grade seven. My dad, he told me if I couldn't get through grade eight by the time I was sixteen I should try something different so he took me into the woods."

"The woods?"

"Lumber camps. My dad worked there. He talked to the foreman and they put me on odd jobs. I've been on odd jobs ever since." He laughed.

"What was it like, working in the woods?"

"Pretty good. In the summer. Not in the winter or the spring or the fall. Ten years of that was enough for me so I come back to town and got a job here. No blackflies, no mosquitoes. Just the priests buzzing around." That laugh again.

I finished my smoke. "Better get going."

———

"Lose your way, Mr. Clemson?" The Pear took one look at me, then got busy scribbling a slip. He held it out between finger and thumb. "Perhaps you'll be good enough to show up in detention room right after classes."

Three minutes late for class and an hour's detention. It was going to be one of those days.

I managed to get through Bartlett's religious studies class while he was talking about priests turning savages into Christians. Art was a snap. Brother Julius had us doing still-life drawing. Gym was gym. Father Prince had us running back and forth getting all sweaty, trying to climb ropes dangling from the ceiling, push-ups, sit-ups.

Science was one class too many.

"Mr. Clemson, are you with us?"

"Huh?" Guys were snickering and giggling.

"A particularly difficult day, Mr. Clemson?"

"Yes, Father."

"Well, if you can just focus on the finish line, Mr. Clemson, I'd like you to answer one final question for the day."

"I'll give it a shot."

More laughter. Father Dyer was not smiling, however. He was headed my way from the front of the class.

"Stand up, Mr. Clemson."

I was standing by the time he reached my desk. He was just about nose to nose with me and he was definitely not happy.

"Describe the major postulates of the cell theory, Mr. Clemson."

"The cell theory?" My brain was numb.

"You have been with us this past week, Mr. Clemson?"

"Yes."

"Yes, Father."

"Yes, Father."

"Mr. Henderson. Would you mind helping Mr. Clemson." Henderson jumped to his feet. Suckhole.

"Yes, Father. Cells. All living things are made up of cells. Cells are the functional units of life."

"Thank you, Mr. Henderson." Henderson sat down, smirking. "Cells are indeed the functional units of life. But it would seem that Mr. Clemson's brain cells are not functioning this afternoon." So lame, but it got more giggles.

"Let's try another question, shall we?"

Father Dyer was still nose to nose with me. His breath stunk of garlic and something else. Gross.

"What is mitosis, Mr. Clemson?"

"Bad breath?"

Bad move.

"Hold your hand out."

"Which one?"

Dyer grabbed my right hand with his left, hauled the strap out of the pocket of his robe, raised his arm and brought the strap down full force on my palm.

Man. Nothing hurts more than that first whack. He gave me two more on that hand, then three on the left, pocketed his strap, then grabbed me by the ear and hauled me out of the classroom and into the time-out room. He shut the light and shut the door.

I sat on my hands. It helped a little, but not much.

Of all the things I hated about St. Iggy's, The Dungeon rated right up there. Once that door closed and the light went out, man. The chair was made of wood — straight back, no cushion — and there was no way you could sit for more than five minutes without starting to squirm around. I usually sat in the corner, leaning against the wall. Close your eyes, open your eyes, it was all the same. Pitch-black except for the little slice of light at the bottom of the door. Now and then you could hear voices from the classrooms and between classes the sound of kids going by in the hallway, laughing and talking. Then silence. Nothing. It was like you'd been dropped into a pit. After a while your mind started playing tricks on you. You heard something scratching around — a rat, maybe, or a mouse — and once you started hearing things like that you were pretty well screwed. Next thing you'd think you could feel something bumping into you or crawling up your leg.

One guy went crazy, screaming and yelling there was a snake in the room and when they opened the door he was frothing at the mouth. They had to take him to the infirmary and he stayed there for days. They finally carted him off to the mental ward at the hospital. His parents had to come and take him away.

The Dungeon really screwed with your mind. No question about it.

"Just like prison," Klemski said. "That's why they put

all the hard cases in solitary. They do it to break you. Send you right over the edge."

"The secret," said Cooper, "is to imagine you're somewhere else. That's what I do. When that door closes, I'm on that beach in British Columbia, staring out at the ocean, going for a swim, fishing, lying in the sun. Try it."

Once Dyer shut the door and the light and I'd made my way to the corner and sat down on my hands I imagined I was in my dad's '56 Ford convertible, white-and-blue two-tone, whitewalls, the works. I loved that car.

Next thing you know, me and my dad had hooked up the boat trailer and were heading out of town to the campground where we went every twenty-fourth of May. Boys' weekend, we called it.

The campground was out on the lake, about forty minutes out of town. We had the top down, like we always did whether it was freezing or not. When we got there, we pitched the tent, rolled out our sleeping bags, set up the camp stove. Then we went down to the ramp and launched the boat, headed out to do a little fishing. We weren't out there five minutes when I caught a nice-looking trout. Then my dad caught one and I caught another and then we headed back, cleaned the fish, fired up the camp stove, had a little feast. Once it was dark, we got the fire pit going, sat on a log and roasted marshmallows.

The whole time — in the car, out in the boat, sitting by

the fire — we were talking. Yak yak yak. I was telling him about stuff me and my friends were up to. He was telling me about the latest house he was building, a great big place for Dr. Johns down on the shore, told me he'd have to take me down to have a look. Finally we couldn't keep our eyes open, so we crawled into our bags and went to sleep.

I must have nodded off, dreamt all that about our camping trip. But suddenly I was awake, and man did I have to go.

That was the worst, when you had to go to the john. You could bang on the door until you broke all the bones in both hands but there was no way the priests would let you out of there before they felt like it. Sometimes you had to do what you had to do, but even in the pitch-black it was embarrassing and the smell was something you don't want to imagine, especially if you had to do something more serious than take a piss. And the priests always seemed to get a big kick out of calling other boys to the doorway to watch you cleaning up.

"Maybe we should get you some diapers the next time, Mr. Clemson."

Maybe you should just go fuck yourself, Father.

There was never a time limit for getting out of The Dungeon. The priest came back and opened the door when he felt like it, or when he remembered that he'd locked you up in the first place.

I was lucky. Dyer remembered where he'd put me, but I'd missed supper.

"Sorry about your luck, Mr. Clemson. But breakfast isn't that far off." I could have killed him on the spot with my bare hands. "Off to bed, Mr. Clemson. Sweet dreams."

I made a beeline for the john. From there, straight to the phone booth on the main floor, just across from the office. I stepped in and shut the door, picked up the receiver and waited for the operator.

I told her I wanted to make a collect call. I wanted to tell my mother about Sullivan. I wanted to tell her about The Dungeon and the freaky priests sneaking around the dorm with their flashlights late at night. I wanted to tell her to spring me out of this madhouse before someone killed me, or I killed someone.

I gave the operator our number.

"Your name?"

I told her, and waited. The phone rang twice. Henry answered.

"You have a collect call from Teddy Clemson. Will you accept the charges?"

"No." Henry hung up.

"I'm sorry sir, but — "

I hung up.

"Bastard."

———

I WAS JUST in time for showers. Same routine as usual. Prince standing guard in the doorway between the locker room and the shower room. Same drooling look in his beady little eyes.

He was a creepy, creepy man. When you had your back to him it was almost as if you could feel his eyes on your ass. When you turned around, it was worse.

"He's always crotch-shopping," Klemski said one day out in the yard. "It's like he's at the buffet, deciding which dish to try."

"Yum, yum," said Anderson.

We laughed. Nervous laughs. That was out in the yard. Nobody laughed in the showers.

Forty minutes after showers, most of the kids sleeping, those same creepy rubber-soled footsteps that I heard every night, flashlight scanning each bed.

Then he came to Cooper's bed. He tapped Cooper with his yardstick, whispered, "Come with me." Waited. When Cooper didn't move, Prince tapped him harder. "Come with me, Cooper. Now."

Cooper threw off the covers, reached under the pillow for his glasses, put them on, stood up and followed Prince out of the dorm, bare feet slapping the floor.

The door swung shut behind him.

3

SEPTEMBER CAME AND went. You couldn't say the same for Cooper. Middle of October, he was still ghosting around, but he wasn't the same Cooper. Ever since Prince started calling him out at night, he'd changed. Sometimes he'd hang around, sometimes he wouldn't. Sometimes he'd talk, other times you couldn't get two sentences out of him. Go out of your way to find him, sit with him and have a smoke, you never knew which Cooper you were going to find.

"You okay, Cooper?"

"Yeah," he said. "I'm fine."

Lousy liar. Even Saturdays didn't cheer him up, and Saturday was the best day of the week. Saturday morning was like any other morning — wake up, chapel, breakfast — except after that we had two hours of study hall and then we were free until supper time.

You could tell Saturday was different as soon as the guard priest opened the door and flipped on the lights. By then some guys had already finished making their beds and were half dressed. Cooper, though, was still just a lump under the covers. The priest — The Pear this morning — gave him a rap on the ass with his yardstick.

"Rise and shine, Mr. Cooper." Cooper mumbled something. Bartlett grabbed the blanket that Cooper had hauled over his head and ripped it right off the bed. "Up, Mr. Cooper. Now!"

Fifteen minutes later, The Pear was marching us to a classroom just down the hall from the chapel.

"Enjoy your reflections," he said. "Brother Joseph will be along presently. And I'd better not hear a sound out of this room." He shut the door.

Klemski's cousin had come through. Thanks to a letter from him threatening legal action, Klemski didn't have to go to religion class anymore, and the rest of the pagans got sprung from chapel.

"Thanks, Klemski. This is just great." This was Campbell, slouching in his desk, chewing a toothpick. "Now we get to sit here and stare at the blackboard for half an hour. At least in chapel we could listen to all that weird stuff they chant."

"That's exactly the point," said Klemski. "They want you to start to like all that weird shit. And as soon as you start asking questions about it, wham." He slammed his palm against the desk. "They spring the trap."

"What trap?"

"The conversion trap, you moron. Ask a couple of questions, then it's, 'Well, Mr. Campbell, if you'd care to learn more, we'd be happy to instruct you.' Next thing you know you'll be carrying beads around and crossing yourself and praying to plaster statues."

"Hey, Klemski." This was Hatfield at the back of the room.

"What?"

"If your cousin can spring us out of chapel, how come he can't spring you out of this hellhole?"

"My mother told him to leave me right where I was. Said maybe the priests could work a miracle. Get rid of my shitty attitude."

"Doesn't seem to be working so far."

Cooper was at the back of the room working on his nails. He'd been doing it for a couple of weeks. Not nibbling. Biting and chewing like a madman. His nails were right down to the quick and he was still going at them. Now he was working on the skin around the edges. His fingers were a mess — red, raw and bleeding.

"Jeezus, Cooper, what are you doing?"

He gave me a spacey look. "Huh?"

"Your fingers."

He looked down at them, turned his hands over and curled his fingers so they were all in a row. Inspected them.

Found one to his liking and began working on it, gnawing at the skin at the top of the nail.

I slid into the desk beside his. He made like he hadn't noticed, but then a minute or so later he looked at me.

"What's the worst thing you ever did?"

"Jeezus, Cooper, where do you get these questions? Give me a minute."

"If you take more than a minute, you're bullshitting me. The worst ones are right at the front of your brain. Can't ever forget them." Gave me the old Cooper grin. Went back to nibbling one of his fingers. "Go on," he said, "I promise not to be shocked."

"One time, I beat the shit out of a kid who was half my size."

"Not bad," said Cooper. "What else?"

"I dunno."

"Yes, you do."

"How do you know?"

"You had to do something worse than that."

"All right, smartass. What's the worst thing you ever did?"

"I cursed God," said Cooper.

"Why?"

"For giving me such a shitty life." That grin again.

"You get hit by a bolt of lightning, or what?"

"Nope. But the shit's been raining down on me ever

since." He gave a little shrug. Then he put his head down on his arms and made like he was having a nap.

For the next half hour we just killed time. Hatfield tried another of his lame jokes.

"What do you call a boomerang that doesn't come back?"

"Beats me," said Klemski.

"A stick." Hatfield put himself in stitches.

"Jeezus, Hatfield," said Campbell. "That is truly awful."

A couple of guys were playing cards. Some were reading. A few had their heads down on their desks, trying to get a little more sleep. Bro Joe came from wherever he'd been.

"All right, boys. Chapel's over. Chow time." We let out a little cheer and herded for the door.

Same crappy food. I was looking forward to lunch — one of Freddy's burnt bus-stop burgers and one of Rita's shakes — so I just went with a couple of pieces of toast. The toast was cold and limp.

Jeezus. You'd think they could at least get the toast right.

"Mind?" I said. I was standing beside Cooper, eyeing the chair beside his.

"Be my guest."

I put my tray beside his and sat down.

He was pushing his eggs around the plate with a fork. He'd chewed the corner off a piece of toast, had maybe a mouthful of eggs. That was it.

"What's up, Cooper?"

He turned, one eye focused on me, the other one looking over my shoulder. He looked back down at his food. Started shoving the eggs around again.

"I was thinking about my dad," he said. "On my tenth birthday my dad was supposed to come and get me. We were going fishing. I was so excited I could hardly sleep. I kept getting up to check my tackle box. Open it up, move things around, close it up. I had the box and my rod by the door of my room for a week before my birthday. That morning I got up around six, got dressed, carried everything out to the front step.

"I was still there at noon. My mother yelled at me to come in out of the sun before I fried my brains. 'That useless piece of shit ain't comin', Timmy. Get your ass in here.' She didn't even wish me happy birthday. Probably didn't even know it was my birthday. One day just drifted into the next for her, all a blur of drugs and booze and boyfriends. Then one day the cops came and took her and her loser friends away. That was it for home. It was foster homes after that, and then group homes, and then here."

"Your old man never came back?"

"Never saw him again."

"Your mom?"

"Haven't seen her in maybe two years. She asked to see me one time. My worker took me over. Mom was flaked out on the couch. No shirt, no pants, just her panties. Bottles and pizza boxes all over the place. Some guy passed out buck naked on the floor. The worker got me out of there in a hurry, said, 'That's no place for you, honey.'"

He dropped his fork on top of the eggs, shoved the plate away.

"No one's gonna miss me when I'm gone," he said, almost in a whisper.

Sometimes when people say things like that they're looking for sympathy, hoping you'll say something dumb like, 'Hey, that can't be true.' But the look on Cooper's face left you with nothing to say because you just knew from the look of him that it was true.

How come a nice kid like Cooper wound up with such assholes for parents?

Cooper pushed his chair back and stood up. Didn't even grunt goodbye.

I finished my toast. Took my time. Cooper wouldn't be too hard to find. Fifteen minutes later, there he was down on his haunches, ass about an inch above the pavement, back against the school wall, him and Wordsworth. He was scribbling something in the margin. Closed the book when I sat down beside him.

I lit him a smoke and handed it over, lit one for myself.

"You're welcome," I said.

"Go fuck yourself."

"Dick the size of mine, that's a bit tricky."

He smiled. "Thanks." He drew on his cigarette. "Sorry," he said. "I'm not in a very good mood."

"I noticed."

"I've been thinking about a lot of bad stuff."

"Your parents?"

"Them. And other stuff."

"What kind of stuff?"

"Stuff," he said.

"Wordsworth help?"

"Wordsworth always helps."

He smiled again. Fiddled with his cigarette.

"Where'd you get that book?"

"Teacher gave it to me. Ed Stevens. Back in grade seven. He was our homeroom teacher. He was really neat. He'd come into class in the morning reciting poetry. You could hear him coming down the hall. Some of the kids made fun of him at first. But after a while, everyone just shut up and listened for him. By the time he walked into the class, the only sound was the sound of his voice. He had a great voice." Cooper dropped his voice down. "Like this." He laughed. "He was amazing. He knew all kinds of stuff off by heart. It made you want to read it, just listening to him. Wordsworth was one of his favorites.

"What though the radiance which was once so bright
Be now forever taken from my sight,
Though nothing can bring back the hour
Of splendour in the grass, of glory in the flower;
We will grieve not, rather find
Strength in what remains behind . . ."

"What is that?"

"It's from *Ode: Intimations of Immortality*. It was one of Mr. Stevens' favorites. He kept reciting bits of it and I kept bugging him to recite more. Finally he just tossed me his book. I took it home and must've read it twenty times that night. Next day I came in and started reciting it. I went to give his book back and he just shook his head. 'It's your book now,' he said.

"The worst thing about that year was, they moved me from one foster home to another and I had to switch schools. Came and got me on a Friday. Monday I was in a new school. I never even got to say goodbye to him." Cooper tossed his cigarette and put his head down on the book on top of his knees.

"Jeezus," he said.

"You want to be alone?"

"Yeah."

I got up and headed for the door.

Cooper was right. About the shit raining down.

———

STUDY HALL WAS torture. Two hours of read a few pages, look at the clock, read a few more pages, look at the clock. There wasn't a sound in the room except for the swish-swish of Sullivan's robes as he snuck up and down the aisles. No one wanted to give him any excuse to send them to The Dungeon. There was nothing he seemed to love more than to catch at least one culprit and totally put the screws to his Saturday.

No luck today. We were all as good as choirboys and then we were saved by the bell.

Fifteen minutes later, I was at the counter of Rita's diner.

"Hey, there, killer. You've survived?"

"So far."

"Don't see too many bruises."

I smiled. "Want me to take my shirt off?"

"I'll take your word for it. What'll it be?"

"One of Freddy's famous burgers and one of your famous shakes. Vanilla. Please."

"Well, they haven't beat the manners out of you yet."

"They'll be the next to go."

"Hey, Freddy," said Rita.

"Way ahead of you, Rita. Burger's already on." Freddy looked through the window. "Fries with that?"

"Please."

"Comin' right up."

"So, what've they been teaching you up there on Prison Hill."

"Never piss off a priest."

"So I hear." Rita was working on the shake. Three scoops of ice cream this time. She ran the metal container up under the thing that spun around and pressed the button. A couple of minutes later, she put the container and a tall glass in front of me, poured the glass full and stuck in a couple of straws.

I took a sip. "Better than ever, Rita."

She gave me one of those smiles. A bit of lipstick on her front teeth. She sat on her stool, pushed a strand of hair away from her face, relit her smoke and waited for Freddy to finish up with the burger and fries.

"Freddy. You still awake back there?"

"Movin' as fast as I can."

"I got a kid out here just fainted from hunger."

"Funny, Rita. Real funny."

The burger was burnt and the fries were still soggy. But everything was hot.

"Hear they had to take some kid to hospital," said Rita. "A week or so ago. Took him out by ambulance in the middle of the night."

"How'd you hear?"

"Ambulance boys come in here pretty regular. Said they had to make a run down to the city. Took the kid to the hospital down there. Said he was talkin' gibberish to himself the whole way down there. Something about snakes. They had to tie him down to the stretcher. Spooked them right out."

I worked on my burger, finished my fries.

"What else has been happening up there?" she said. I told her about Cruickshank getting banged against the wall, Cooper and me being tossed in The Dungeon.

Rita shook her head.

"What I'd like to know is," I said, "how come they get away with all that stuff?"

"Those guys are in a world of their own. It's like they got a moat around the place. They get away with stuff that would land most people in jail."

"How come?"

"They're priests. No one messes with the Church. Not the cops. No one."

———

I'D BEEN UP one side of Main Street and back down the other when a pickup pulled to the curb beside me.

"Well, say." Rozey's shiny smiling face.

"Hey, Rozey."

"You got plans or are you just passing the time?"

"No plans," I said. "There isn't a whole lot to do in a place like this."

"You can say that again."

"There isn't a whole lot to do in a place like this."

Rozey laughed, leaned across and opened the door.

"Wanna go for a ride?"

Rozey's pickup was an old Ford, blue and beat up. There were boxes and tires and old cans and junk in the back. The dashboard was littered with scraps of paper and old coffee cups. There was a toolbox on the floor, and a pair of old work boots, one running shoe and a tackle box, a set of booster cables, a scraper for the windshield.

"Shove that stuff over," said Rozey. I shoved the tackle box and the toolbox over until I had enough room for my feet. Then I climbed in and shut the door.

"Mind if I smoke?"

"Not if you're sharin'."

We lit up and Rozey put the truck in gear and pulled out onto Main Street.

"Where to?" I said.

"Nowhere in particular. I was just out drivin' around, seein' what's what."

"What's what so far?"

"Not much," said Rozey. He picked up his coffee cup from the dash and took a sip, put the cup back.

"Looks like you live in this thing."

He laughed. "Bought her new in '52. Haven't cleaned her out since. My girlfriend doesn't care."

"Your girlfriend?"

He pointed at the air freshener hanging from the mirror. A picture of a girl in a bathing suit.

"She never says nothin' about the mess." He laughed.

We drove down Main Street to the end. There was a town, and suddenly no town, just rocks and bush. We drove out of town maybe five minutes and Rozey turned down a side road.

"What's down here?"

"The shopping center," said Rozey.

Five minutes later, we came to a cutoff on the left. The sign said BELLEVIEW MUNICIPAL LANDFILL.

"The dump?"

Rozey laughed. "Pretty near everyone comes out here shopping. Great bargains." We parked on a rise overlooking the pit. Rozey cut the engine.

Big pit about as long as a football field. One end was filled with washers and dryers and old fridges, car engines, car wheels, entire hulks of rusted-out cars and pickups, chesterfields and chairs, old lamps. At the other end there were mounds and mounds of garbage. From where we were sitting the smell wasn't too bad, but on a hot day with the wind blowing at you it would be a killer.

"You come out here often?"

"Oh, yeah," said Rozey. "At least once a week. Sometimes more often, depending."

"On what?"

"How much good stuff there is to pick through."

"You pick through the trash?"

"Nope. Just the good stuff."

"Like what?"

"Oh, boy. Lots of stuff. I got a good washer and dryer out of here last year. All they needed was a bit of cleaning up, bang out the dents. Took me a while, but they work just great. People are always comin' around to my place lookin' for bargains." He laughed.

"This lady come by one time, just nosin' around the barn and she saw this armchair. Real nice one. I'd fixed one arm and reupholstered it. Wasn't perfect, but wasn't bad. 'I had one just like this, only a different color,' she says. 'What happened to it?' I says. 'My kid sat on the arm and busted it right off. Took it out to the dump.' 'Which arm?' I says. 'Left one,' she says. She paid me twenty bucks. I carried the chair out to her truck and put it in the back and she drove off with her same old chair." He laughed again.

"Hey!" he said. He pointed at a clearing on the far side of the pit.

Holy shit. A black bear was just nosing out of the

bush on the rim of the pit right across from us.

"They can't see very good, but they can pick up a scent a mile away. If she smells us she'll take off."

She sniffed the air and then ambled down the slope and into the pit.

"Lunch time," said Rozey.

She worked the trash, clawing through the piles until she found something she liked.

We watched her for maybe five minutes.

"Here comes her boyfriend."

Another bear came out of the bush, looked about twice her size, paused a moment before skidding down the bank and into the pit.

"This is neat," I said.

"Better than going to the movies. Especially since we don't have a theater." He pronounced it *thee-ate-her*.

We watched the bears for another fifteen minutes or so. Then Rozey fired up the truck. The bears looked up, but they didn't move. We backed away from the rim of the pit and turned around.

"Wanna go see Rozey's Furniture and Appliances?"

"Sure."

Rozey's place was on the far side of town. Down another side road about a mile in from the highway, his house was on a rise, the barn behind it. Neither had been painted for years from the look of it.

"If you paint them, you have to keep on painting every few years. I'm saving money," said Rozey.

"You grow up here?"

"I was born here," said Rozey. "After Mother died, Dad and I lived on here alone. Since he died, it's just me."

We parked behind the house and he led the way to the barn. He opened a side door and stepped inside, flipping on a light.

We were in a kind of workshop: lathe and saws, workbench, tools hanging from hooks and nails hammered into the wall. Scattered around the room there were stoves and fridges, washers and dryers and all kinds of furniture — tables and chairs, framed mirrors, sofas, desks, you name it.

"You get all this from the dump?"

"Mostly."

"And people come out and buy it?"

"Oh, yeah," said Rozey. "They say I should put a sign out by the road. Rozey's Antiques. Only problem is, there aren't that many tourists and all the locals know where to find me." He opened a back door that led out to the yard. "I want to show you something." Behind the barn there was a big unpainted shed, double doors on the end facing the barn. He unhooked the latch and opened the doors.

Inside, sitting on a wooden cradle on a trailer was a sailboat, maybe thirty feet long. Lots of the planks were missing so you could see right through to the ribs, black and rotten.

"Got it for nothing," said Rozey. "Guy was always going to get around to fixing it up, but never did. Finally his wife told him to fix it up or get rid of it. 'You haul it away, it's yours,' he says. I had it out of there the next afternoon. Know anything about boats?"

"Nope."

"It's a yawl, twenty-six feet. Sleeps four. Has a kitchen and bathroom and everything." He led me to the stern where there was a ladder. He climbed up first, then helped me up onto the deck. He stepped down into the cockpit and then through the hatch and down a little ladder into the cabin.

He sat on one of the bunks, beaming. "Beautiful, eh?"

It would have been, at one time.

There was a kitchen, a couple of cabinet doors missing, and a little counter with a stove. In the middle of the cabin there was a table and an L-shaped bench, the cushions worn and tatty. Looked like some mice were making themselves at home in one of the cushions. Toward the bow were two bunks, then a doorway and two more bunks.

Smelled kind of sad, like rot and mildew.

"How long you had it?"

"About six months. By next summer I'll be sailing."

Seemed like it would take a lot longer than that to fix this thing up. But what did I know?

"Where?"

"Georgian Bay, down through the lakes to the St. Lawrence. Down the St. Lawrence and out into the Atlantic."

"You ever sailed before?"

"Nope."

"And you're going to sail out into the Atlantic?"

"If I can get through all the lakes and locks, the ocean shouldn't be a problem. I'll be a real sailor by then."

He pulled out a road atlas and put it on the table, opened it to a double-page spread that showed all the Great Lakes.

"Here we are, and here's where I'll be going." He traced the route with his index finger. "Down here and through here and along here. I can hardly wait."

He sounded like a big kid.

"You going to use a road map to get there?"

"Yeah." Beamed me a big smile. "You wanna come along?"

"Maybe," I said.

What I was thinking was, good luck with that. Through the Great Lakes, down the St. Lawrence and out into the Atlantic with a map from the local White Rose station?

But it did sound pretty cool, too. Something to think about in The Dungeon, anyway.

"Jeez," said Rozey. He tapped his watch. "Better get you back. The priests hate it when people are late. I don't want them to yell."

Rozey dropped me off on the side street around the corner from St. Iggy's.

"I'd drop you off out front, but we aren't supposed to have nothin' to do with the boys, eh? I could get in trouble."

"No problem, Rozey." I got out. "Thanks." Shut the door.

Rozey waved, put the old Ford in gear and headed off.

There wasn't much more depressing than coming back to St. Iggy's after being sprung free for an afternoon. For a little while, it felt like I had a normal life again.

Just before supper, it was mail call. We all filed into the study hall where one of the priests — Docherty, usually — was at the front with the mail bag on the desk. Once we were all seated and everyone had shut up, he started with the air mail.

Docherty was a skinny little guy. Black hair slicked back. Wasn't too old, not like a lot of the other priests. He'd pull a letter out of the bag, call out the person's name, then fire the letter through the air in the general direction of the person who was supposed to get it.

The priests loved it. Some of them, the really mean bastards, liked to fire letters right out the open windows. "Gee, sorry about that, Henderson." If a letter went zipping out the window you had to wait until mail call was over to go find it. For the priests it was payback time for all the grief you'd caused them during the week. They didn't seem to remember that stuff about turning the other cheek.

Docherty was just about finished firing all the letters when he called out my name. I put up my hand and he flipped the letter over my head.

"Sorry, Mr. Clemson."

What an asshole. Someone in the back of the room picked up my letter and it got passed back to me.

It was from my mother. I folded it in half and put it in my pocket. The rule was you couldn't open your mail until all the letters and parcels had been delivered.

Docherty held the bag upside down and shook it.

"That's it, boys."

Cooper got up out of his chair and headed for the door. No mail for Cooper. No mail for Cooper since we'd shown up at St. Iggy's. From the look on his face it didn't seem to matter one way or the other. But you could never really tell with Cooper. He had a tricky little face.

I went out to the yard and down the fence line to the far end, sat under a spruce tree and opened the letter. My mother had slipped some fives and tens into the envelope. I folded them and put them in my pocket.

Dear Teddy,

Hope everything is going fine up there. Haven't heard

from you. Did the letter get lost in the mail? Ha-ha.
Things are going fine here. Henry and I . . .

Screw Henry. I dropped the letter in the trash bin just outside the door.

Dinner time was always quiet on Saturdays. Being cooped up was that much worse after you'd had the afternoon to wander around town with no priests looking over your shoulder.

I was actually glad to go to bed. I pulled the blanket over my head. Must have been asleep in two minutes flat.

Next thing, I heard the dorm door squeak open. I looked out from under my blanket and there was Cooper silhouetted against the light from the landing. The door swung shut behind him. He headed straight for the washroom. He was in there a long time.

I got up and went in. Cooper's feet in the stall at the end.

"Cooper, you all right?" He didn't say anything.

"Cooper?"

"Fuck off. Leave me alone."

4

ONE DAY, MIDDLE of October, Cooper and I were out in the yard sitting on the ground, our backs against the wall. We had our jacket collars up against the wind. The sky was just a mass of grumpy-looking clouds, all different shades of gray. Storm clouds.

We were having a smoke before morning classes. Cooper kept flicking his cigarette with the tip of his finger.

"I'll tell you this much. I can't take this place much longer."

We could see the cars and trucks heading up the hill out of town, heading west.

"We could break out together," I said. "Head out to the highway, stick out our thumbs. Next thing you know, we'd be at that beach of yours out in B.C."

"I dream about that beach." Cooper was flicking the lid of his lighter, snapping it shut, flipping it open. "It's what gets me through my time in The Dungeon. I saw a picture of it once. A rocky beach with big logs all over the place. They float in from the ocean. That's what the people use to build their shacks."

"They live right there on the beach?"

"Up at the edge of the bush that comes down to the beach. They go surfing and swimming. Spend their days just hanging around doing what they want. They go fishing for their dinner and grow things in clearings above the beach. They get their water from a stream. They don't need jobs because they don't need money. Everything they need they've got right there. Paradise, brother."

"How long do you figure it would take us to get there?"

"A week if we got lucky with rides, if we got on with a trucker who was heading straight through. Couple of weeks otherwise. But who gives a shit? As long as we're on the road."

We sat there for quite a few minutes just looking at the cars and trucks disappearing over the top of the hill.

I nudged him with my elbow. "Well, what's keeping us?"

He didn't answer. He lit up another smoke.

He'd just pocketed his lighter when O'Hara and his pack of nitwits came around the corner. O'Hara looked at his buddies and then down at Cooper. Wicked smile.

"How's the Little Prince?"

There are assholes in every school and in St. Iggy's we had more than our share. O'Hara was a grade ten weenie.

Parted his hair in the middle and pasted it down on either side with Brylcreem. Way too much Brylcreem. He had a little piggy nose and little piggy eyes. You just wanted to smack him as soon as you saw him.

Cooper looked up at him, and then at the pack behind him. If O'Hara had had any brains he would have shut up and moved on. But when they were handing out brains he thought they said trains and he got on the wrong one.

"Have fun last night?"

Cooper was on him before O'Hara knew what hit him.

I'd never seen Cooper in action before, but he was something to see. O'Hara was a mess of blood and snot and tears, and the blood just seemed to make Cooper go wild. He was kneeling on O'Hara, pinning both arms with his knees and he just hammered him. Left, right. Left, right.

"Enough!"

Who knew where Father Sullivan came from, but he had Cooper by the jacket and hauled him off O'Hara who was blubbering like a baby. Sullivan turned Cooper around so that he was facing him.

"What do you think you're doing?"

"Beating the crap out of him."

O'Hara had managed to sit up. His nose and mouth were a mess.

"He just jumped me, Father. I was minding my own business and he jumped me. He's crazy."

"That's not true," I said. "O'Hara started it."

"You stay out of this." Sullivan wasn't in the mood to get to the bottom of things. He just grabbed Cooper by the arm, hauled him inside and shoved him in the nearest dungeon.

O'Hara had managed to get to his knees. I was standing right in front of him. He was wiping his nose and mouth with the sleeve of his shirt. He looked up at me.

"What the fuck are you looking at?"

"You, you retard. You make one more smartass crack to Cooper and after he beats the shit out of you, I'll finish you off."

"Fuck you."

"You wanna go, right now?" I gave him a swift kick in the ribs. "Let's go. Right now, asshole." He looked around for his buddies. They had pulled the vanishing act. O'Hara got up and ran for the door.

Such a chickenshit.

I sat back down where Cooper and I had been sitting. I lit up a smoke. My hands were shaking, I was so pissed.

Next thing, I was looking at a pair of size tens and there was Mather.

"What happened?"

"O'Hara was being an asshole."

"He's always being an asshole. He was born an asshole. Then he took lessons. What'd he do to Cooper?"

I told him.

"That little prick." Mather turned and walked off.

———

SAY THIS ABOUT Father Dunlop. He was the easiest guy at St. Iggy's to derail. Ask him a question about geography and no matter what he was intending to do during class, he'd be off on a wild goose chase. We'd take turns seeing if we could keep him off topic for an entire class. We did it twice.

Cooper had twisted my brain talking about his beach. I shot up my hand, asked Dunlop about Vancouver Island.

"It's very mountainous," he said. "There's a ridge of mountains pretty well from one end of the island to the other. Some pretty big mountains, too. Give me a second."

He turned to his bookshelf, ran a finger along the spines until he found the book he was looking for. Took another couple of minutes flipping pages.

"Yes," he said. "It's almost three hundred miles long and about fifty miles across. A pretty big island. The tallest mountain . . ."

There was a knock on the door. Dunlop went over and opened it.

"Ah, Mr. Rozell." Rozey came in carrying a stepladder.

"This one right here," said Dunlop, pointing to the dead light over his desk. Rozey set up his ladder.

"Where was I?" said Dunlop.

Someone chirped out from the back. "Vancouver Island."

Dunlop went on for a few minutes about some of the things he'd done out there: whale watching, fishing, hiking. He'd seen eagles and bears and, just once, a cougar.

Rozey was fiddling with the globe over the lightbulb. There was a little screw thing you had to undo. Then the globe came off. He climbed down the ladder and set it on Dunlop's desk. Then he climbed back up and unscrewed the bulb, climbed back down and set it on the desk.

"How many men does it take to change a lightbulb?" This was Henderson, leaning over and whispering. I shrugged. "One," he said. "But it could take all day."

I gave Henderson the glare. Whispered, "Shut up, asshole."

"You were saying something, Mr. Clemson?"

"No, Father."

Rozey looked at the bulb he'd taken out, and the one he'd brought to replace it.

"Sorry, Father. I brought the wrong one. I'll be right back."

Henderson snickered. Rozey headed out the door.

I asked Dunlop about the beaches.

Dunlop watched Rozey go, then turned to face us.

"The beaches. Yes, the beaches. They're mostly pebbles and rocks. They call them cobble beaches. You need to wear running shoes to walk along them. They tend to be piled with driftwood, and during the winter there are wonderful storms. Waves ten, twenty, thirty feet high crashing ashore. They pick up those driftwood logs and toss them around like matchsticks. It's quite a sight." He paused, and it looked like he was remembering it all from a long time ago.

"You should go there some day, Mr. Clemson. You would be enthralled."

A couple of the guys at the back giggled. I turned around and told them to shut up. I felt bad for Dunlop. He made himself an easy target with words like that but he was a pretty decent guy. I turned back around and put up my hand.

"Is it true that you can live on those beaches year round?"

"That's what they say. It's a very temperate climate." He looked at me and smiled. "Thinking about it, Mr. Clemson?"

"Yeah," I said. "One of these days I might give it a try."

———

I WAS IN NO mood for The Pear's religion class. We were

talking about God's grand design. I put up my hand.

"Yes, Mr. Clemson."

"Does anything happen without God knowing about it?"

"No, Mr. Clemson," said Bartlett. "God knows about everything. Even your innermost thoughts. Which is why you might choose to be careful what you're thinking."

"So he's spying on us all the time?"

"I wouldn't say he was spying, Mr. Clemson. More like keeping a watchful eye."

"So he sees everything?"

"Yes, he does. Even the little sparrow who falls."

"What about when an innocent person is killed. Like accidentally being in the wrong place at the wrong time. Maybe crossing the street and gets hit by a car. Could God have seen that coming?"

"Of course. God sees everything."

"Well, if the person was innocent, was just walking into it, why wouldn't God save him?"

"God works in mysterious ways, Mr. Clemson. We never really know why he does what he does."

"Suppose someone who should be protecting you, taking care of you, decides to take advantage of you. Decides to hurt you."

"Do you have an example in mind?"

"Suppose a father decides to beat up a kid. Does God see that?"

"Yes."

"Why would God allow that to happen?"

"Sometimes it's difficult to discern God's grand design. We just have to be assured that he knows what he's doing."

"Even when he lets fathers hurt kids?"

Bartlett got a weird look on his face. "I think we've taken this as far as we can today. It's time to move along. And Mr. Clemson has inadvertently paved the way." He gave me The Look. "Let's talk about the proper way to pray in order to ensure that the good Lord hears our petitions."

What a load of crap.

———

"Hey, Clemson." Hatfield was running up the hall and then fell in beside me. "Why do bees hum?"

"I have no fucking idea, Hatfield. Why do bees hum?"

"Because they don't know the words."

"That's horrible, Hatfield."

"Yeah," he said. "I know."

We turned the corner and there was Prince standing in the doorway of the gym.

"Move it, gentlemen. We haven't got all day."

He was always a bastard in gym class, but today was worse than usual. He was barking orders from the time we got into the gym until the time we left. Nothing anyone did was good enough. When he was in a mood like that, all you did was work as hard as you could so you wouldn't give him an excuse to give you a detention or send you to The Dungeon.

It worked for most of us. But it wasn't Klemski's day. Leave it to a prick like Prince to pick on a poor lump like Klemski.

"Grab the rope."

Klemski looked at the rope, and then at Prince. He knew he was doomed. There was no way he could haul his ass three feet up that rope, never mind get himself all the way to the ceiling and back down.

"Go!"

Klemski gave it his best shot. His face turned pink and then red and almost purple as he tried to haul himself up. His feet never got more than two feet off the mat.

"You're pathetic, Klemski. You know that?"

Klemski didn't say anything.

"Did you hear me, Klemski?"

Klemski dropped to the floor. "Yes, Father."

"Is that 'Yes, Father, I heard you,' or 'Yes, Father, I know that I'm pathetic.'"

Klemski looked at Prince the way he'd look down the barrel of a loaded gun.

"Both, I guess."

"You guess?" Prince turned to look for another victim.

My turn. I grabbed the rope and managed to get maybe five feet off the floor before my arms gave out. I dropped to the mat.

"Mr. Clemson."

I couldn't stand to look at him. It gave me the creeps. I just looked down at the mat.

"Look at me when I'm talking to you, Clemson."

I looked at him.

"Who said you could stop climbing?"

"I couldn't go up any further."

"Try again. Now."

It was even worse this time. I got up three, maybe four feet, and just dangled there.

Prince was in a rage.

"You are all pathetic. All of you. And I won't tolerate an entire class of pathetic weaklings. For the next four weeks we are going to do nothing other than chin-ups, push-ups and sit-ups. You are going to get in shape even if it kills you."

I dropped to the mat.

"Starting now. Everyone down."

For the rest of the class we sweated it out. Sit-ups, push-ups, chin-ups, while Prince marched up and down yelling at us and insulting us. It wouldn't have taken much for all of us to jump on him like a pack of dogs.

"Pathetic," he yelled. "Repeat after me. 'I am pathetic, Father.'"

We repeated it.

"Louder!"

We hollered it out. He made us keep chanting it until the bell went.

"Get out of my sight!" The veins in his neck were bulging.

Jesus God.

————

WE WERE ALMOST done for the day. Father Dyer was humming on about the periodic table. Another twenty minutes to go, then free time in the yard, except for the guys who'd gotten detentions.

Suddenly, the fire alarm started ringing. Dyer was startled, looked up at the big red bell on the wall as if he didn't quite believe what he was hearing. People herded for the door.

"Single file! Single file!"

By the time we got down two flights and out the door, we could hear the sirens. A few guys cheered and whistled. This was definitely better than the periodic table. Before Dyer got out the door, we were all around at the front of the building — all two hundred of us — cheering and applauding when the fire trucks arrived. The priests were doing their best to get us to stand back, as if maybe the whole building might blow up before our eyes. Father Stewart was standing near the front doors, waiting for the fire crew.

"The basement," he said. "The laundry room."

The firemen hooked up their hose to the hydrant on the front lawn and headed inside. They were in there quite a while. We all just stood around. There was the usual pushing and shoving and screwing around. The priests were too preoccupied with the fire to worry about us.

The firemen opened a couple of basement windows and smoke started pouring out.

Finally the smoke thinned out. A little while after that, the firemen emerged.

Whistles and applause. It took them a while to roll up their hoses. The chief was over by the front door talking with Stewart. We couldn't hear what they were saying. Stewart shook the chief's hand and watched him go. Then he looked at us.

"Everyone into the gym. Now!"

Cooper and I were way back at the end of the line, and the line was just inching along. No one was in a hurry to hear whatever Stewart had to say.

I nudged Cooper, nodded to my left. Mather and Grainger rounded the corner. A couple of minutes later, O'Hara came around the end of the building, heading for the line. What Cooper had started, Mather and Grainger finished. O'Hara's left eye was swollen shut. His mouth was all bloody.

Brother Wilbur spotted him, grabbed him by the shoulder. "What happened to you?"

"I fell."

People started laughing. Brother Wilbur gave us the evil eye. "Keep moving, gentlemen." He turned back to O'Hara. "Go to the infirmary. Get yourself looked at."

O'Hara shook his head. "I'll be all right."

Wilbur shrugged. "Suit yourself." He went up the line, trying to get the guys to put a move on.

I turned to look at O'Hara. "Every asshole gets his due," I said.

O'Hara gave me The Look with his one good eye. Didn't say anything.

Ten minutes later we were all in the gym, standing at attention. Stewart stood up on the stage. His face was almost purple.

"We are going to hear confessions, gentlemen. Starting with the junior grades and working our way up. Grade nine students will go first. The rest of you will remain here. Those who are not Catholic will go with Brother Joseph to the study hall. We will deal with you in due time."

"They can't do this," said Klemski. He was huffing and puffing his way up the stairs behind me, speaking in a whisper. "Confessions are supposed to be confidential."

"What's the chance no one will confess to setting the fire?" I said.

"Hundred per cent."

"Which means?"

"The pagans are about to be in deep shit."

Klemski was right, as usual.

Stewart came into the study hall about an hour after we'd left the gym. He marched up the middle aisle, then turned to face us.

He was pissed. Capital P.

"Well, gentlemen. It wasn't one of us. Which means it must be one of you. Who threw the cigarette down the laundry chute?"

No hands went up. Stewart took his time, glaring at one face after another. Still no volunteer.

"We have all the time in the world, gentlemen. You will remain here until the culprit confesses. If it takes all night, so be it."

It took all night.

Try that some time. Sitting on a hard seat attached to a desk. You can slide down until the back of your head is almost resting on the back of the chair, but ten minutes of that and the back of your head is killing you. Then you can sit up straight and just stare at the board and then you can cross your arms on your desk and put your head down. But you can't do any one of them for more than fifteen minutes.

The priests knew all about torture. Must've learned from the Indians who put Brébeuf through his final paces.

But after a couple of hours in study hall, it wasn't the priests I was thinking of killing. It was Henry, that son of a bitch.

I was trying to remember how Henry had managed to squirm his way into our lives in the first place, creepy bastard. One day it's me and Mom and Dad. Then I'm twelve and there's a big scene in the middle of the night and my dad disappears and it's just me and Mom. Then I'm thirteen and Henry's plumping his fat ass down on the sofa and telling me to get him a beer.

"Get your own beer." I headed for my room, slamming the door. He let it pass. But a few months later he'd hung his salesman suits in my father's closet and slipped into my father's side of the bed. He had Mom wrapped around his finger, the one with the big fake diamond pinkie ring.

From then on it was two against one. I spent all the time I could out of the house, hanging around at friends' places, around downtown, in the park. I came home late and left early. The less I saw of Henry and my mother the better. I wouldn't say two words to Henry if I could help it. I froze the bastard right out. But it was only a matter of time before he figured out how to get me out of the house entirely. Scheming, weaselly little bastard. What my mother saw in him with his little salesman's moustache and salesman's paunch and crappy checkerboard salesman's clothes was anyone's guess.

Beats me how she could go from being married to my father to letting a slug like Henry move in. But six months after he first started coming around, he showed up with all his stuff in boxes and bags. I sat there with my feet on the coffee table, a bag of chips in my lap, reading a hot rod magazine. Just watched him huff and puff his way up and down the stairs.

When he was all done, he came over and grabbed my feet and pushed them off the table.

"You don't do that in my house," he said.

I looked at him and then at my mother. She didn't say a word.

Since when did a boyfriend count more than your own son?

I could still hear his voice coming down the phone line like a bullet: "No." And I could just see his smug little smile as he hung up the phone. I could see him turning to my mother with a shrug: "Wrong number."

He could shove the phone where the sun don't shine.

But the one who really pissed me off was my father. Where'd that bastard get to, anyway? Me and Cooper had that much in common. Disappearing fathers.

I wondered if vanishing fathers ever stopped for a minute before they dropped their drawers and jumped into bed with their new girlfriends and thought about how they were totally screwing the lives of everyone they were leaving behind. I had a hard time imagining that my old man ever gave me a second thought. But there wasn't a day went by that I didn't wish I could see him. And there wasn't a day that I didn't think how much I'd love to kill him as soon as I laid eyes on him.

"Bastard."

"Who's a bastard?" Cooper had snuck up on me. I was standing at the windows at the end of study hall. I could see the lights of the cars heading west on the highway out of town.

"My father, for one," I said. "And my mother's sorry excuse for a boyfriend."

"My old lady was a magnet for losers," said Cooper. "They just seemed to crawl out of the sewer and show up at our place all tattoos and B.O. One night I woke up and one of those jerks was in my bed, groping me. I was, like, maybe six years old. I started to struggle, tried to get away and he said, 'One word out of you and I'll kill you,' and I knew he meant it and I had to just lie there and let him do it to me, had to bite my pillow so I wouldn't scream. I was shitting blood for a week after that."

"Holy shit, Cooper."

We stood there for another minute. Cooper was looking out the window.

"Does it ever piss you off?" I said.

"Does what piss me off?"

"How your life turned out."

"Every day," said Cooper. "I can't figure it out. I was only a little kid when my life went all to shit. How bad could I have been to deserve all this? I swore a lot. I set a fire once."

"You didn't deserve it."

"So why all the shit raining down on my head? Some kids wind up in nice homes with nice families. You and me, we wind up in St. Iggy's? What is it, luck of the draw?"

"I guess."

"Well, I wish they'd reshuffle the deck. Let me pick another card."

He was still looking out the window. It was so dark you couldn't really see the highway except when a car went up the hill, tail lights winking and blinking out of sight.

"What I wouldn't give to be in one of those cars." He didn't say anything more for a few minutes. Just kept on looking out the window.

"I thought you were getting out of here, end of September," I said. "What happened?"

"Things changed."

"What things?"

"Things." He walked away, went back to his desk, put his head down on his arms. A few of the other guys were doing the same, but a couple of them had given up on desks and stretched out on the floor. Eyes wide open, staring at the ceiling.

I went back to my desk, put my head down and somehow managed to fall asleep.

Stewart marched in at six in the morning.

"Would the guilty party be willing to admit to setting yesterday's fire?"

No volunteers.

"Very well. Go now and get ready for the day. You will go to classes and at the end of classes you will return to the study hall and you will stay here again all night. You can blame the criminal among you for your discomfort."

Cooper shot up his hand.

"Well," said Stewart. "An honest man at last."

"Did it cross your mind that one of your Catholics might have lied in confession?"

Stewart's face went red. "That's completely out of the question, Cooper, and if you were a Catholic you would understand that."

"They lie about all sorts of other things. Why wouldn't they lie about setting a fire?"

"I won't grace that with a response, Cooper." And he stormed out.

We slept in study hall for four nights running. Stewart finally gave up.

———

THE THING ABOUT St. Iggy's was you could never tell when the sky would start to fall. You knew it was going to happen, but you could never quite tell what would set things off.

All it took the last Saturday in October was bigmouth bully Patrick Stewart picking on his favorite target, Zits Cruickshank. Stewart was a no-neck body-builder senior who was always making life miserable for everyone in grade nine. Zits was gangling his way down the main hallway, head down, a stack of books under his arm. Stewart was coming the other way. He was looking right at Zits and you could tell by the smirk on his face that he had Zits in his sights.

When he got beside Zits, Stewart punched the stack of books Zits had under his arm. Books went flying everywhere.

Zits looked up.

"You fucking sonofabitch, Stewart." Cruickshank looked at his books all over the floor and just lost it. He took a swing at Stewart and missed. Then Stewart took off and Zits took off right behind him. Stewart rounded the corner into the main hallway. You could hear his laughter echoing off the walls as Cruickshank chased him down the hall toward the main office. "Stewart, you fucking prick. I'm going to kill you, you cocksucker."

Which is exactly the moment Father Stewart came out of his office to see what all the noise was about. Cruickshank just about ran right into him. Looked like he wanted to die. His eyes were wide open and his face was red and his pimples were flaming.

"That's the filthiest language I have ever heard. I will not tolerate that kind of language in my school, Mr. Cruickshank." He was standing chest to chest with Cruickshank.

It looked like Cruickshank was going to burst into tears. "Stewart knocked my — "

"We're not talking about Mr. Stewart. We are talking about you and your filthy mouth. Drop your trousers."

"What?" Cruickshank looked at Stewart. He knew exactly what was coming next. We all did.

"Drop your trousers. Now!"

Cruickshank fumbled with his belt, undid the buckle, undid the button, undid his fly, held on to his pants by the waistband.

"Father, I . . ."

"Drop them!"

Cruickshank let go of his pants. They dropped to his ankles.

"Your shorts."

"Father, please . . ."

"Drop your shorts. Now!" Stewart's voice echoed down the hall. Stewart pulled the strap from the pocket in his robe. Cruickshank looked at the strap, then at Stewart. His eyes started to well up. He opened his mouth to say something, but then just dropped his shorts.

"Turn and put your hands against the wall."

"Please, Father, don't . . ."

"Put your hands against the wall."

Cruickshank turned, put his hands against the wall.

"Lower."

Cruickshank lowered his hands so that he was bent at the waist, leaning against the wall. Stewart reached back and swung, caught Cruickshank square on the ass. Sickening sound. Cruickshank screamed. Stewart hit him again and again, raised his hand to hit him once more and Cruickshank screamed again.

"Shut up," said Stewart and brought the strap down even harder. Cruickshank was wailing, couldn't help himself. It just seemed to make Stewart even madder, lashing and lashing until Cruickshank finally just crumpled to the floor, curled up and held his hands over his ass.

"Move your hands. Move them!" Cruickshank left his hands where they were. Stewart leaned down and gave him a whack right on the hands.

Jeezus.

Cruickshank was howling and crying and pleading with Stewart to stop. Stewart gave him another whack on the hands and when Cruickshank pulled his hands away, gave him another one, harder than the others. Cruickshank's ass was raw and bleeding.

"Oh, my God, Father. Please."

"Don't you dare utter the name of the Lord. I won't have that name issuing from the same mouth that spewed such filth. Get up! Get up!"

Cruickshank got to his knees, and then to his feet. He was a mess of snot and tears.

"Pull up your trousers."

Cruickshank pulled up his shorts, then his trousers. It took him a minute to fiddle with the buttons and the fly and the buckle, his hands were so messed up.

"Go and get your toothbrush."

There was a big gang of us gathered in the hallway. Normally Stewart would yell at us to take off, go wherever we were supposed to go. But he just looked at us and didn't say anything. So we all just stood there waiting for Zits to come back with his toothbrush.

"Now, go down to the janitor's closet, fill his bucket with soap and water and come back here." Zits did as he was told, pushing the bucket with the mop that was in it.

"You won't be needing the mop, Mr. Cruickshank. Get down on your hands and knees." Zits got down. "Now, dip your toothbrush into the bucket and start scrubbing. You will scrub this entire hall with your toothbrush, Mr. Cruickshank."

Zits started scrubbing.

"And after you're done scrubbing the hall, you will scrub out your mouth with that toothbrush."

Stewart turned to look at the rest of us.

"Take this as a warning. We will not tolerate filthy language in this institution. Ever. You are to model yourself on Christ's example. Always. Now, get to study hall!" Stewart's voice bounced off the floor and the walls.

We got out of there in a hurry.

As soon as we got around the corner, Klemski looked at me and shook his head.

"Christ's example? Fuck. He's a madman."

All I could think of in study hall was poor Cruickshank and his sorry bleeding ass. For the first half hour, my hands were still shaking. I could see Father Stewart, all wild and out of control.

What kind of a fucking place was this, anyway?

———

IT WAS A BEAUTIFUL day for October, not that Zits would ever find out. The sun was out, there were only a couple of clouds in that blue, blue sky. Bright and chilly but when you weren't walking into the wind you could actually feel the warmth of the sun. Cooper and I had our jackets and toques on but by the time we reached the street, we'd unzipped our jackets and shoved the toques into our pockets.

We crossed the road and headed to the side street where Rozey was always waiting for me.

"Who's the guy who picks you up on Saturdays in that old pickup?"

"Rozey? He's the janitor."

"The retard?"

"He's not a retard," I said. "He's a nice guy." I told him about the boiler room and about all the times I'd gone down there to have a smoke.

"And all this time we thought you were in the john jerking off," Cooper laughed.

We rounded the corner and there was Rozey's truck. He had his elbow out the window and was tapping his fingers against the windowsill. We could hear the music way back at the corner. Buddy Holly. He had the radio cranked right up. *That'll be the day-ay-ay that* ... drifting out of the window.

"Would it be all right if I hung around with you guys?"

"Sure. No problem."

"You wanna ask him?"

"He won't mind."

Rozey was watching us in the rear-view mirror. Just when we pulled even with the back of the truck he reached over and opened the passenger side door. The music was still blaring. He turned down the volume.

"Hi, guys."

"Rozey, this is my friend, Cooper."

Rozey smiled one of his big smiles and extended his hand.

"Hey, Cooper." Cooper reached in and shook Rozey's hand. "Jump in." Cooper got in and slid over beside Rozey and I got in beside him and slammed the door.

"Mind if Cooper hangs around with us today?"

"Yeah," said Rozey. "I mind like crazy. Kick that shit out of the way and make some room for yourself, Cooper." He threw the truck in gear and we idled off down the street. Cooper cleared some room for his feet. He looked at Rozey and then at me. He looked like a kid who just got on the roller coaster at the carnival. Big shit-eating grin.

We turned onto Rozey's side road, gravel chattering in the wheel wells, then turned into his drive and jounced up the hill. Rozey stopped in front of the barn, shut the engine.

Rozey gave Cooper the grand tour. We went through the barn and into Rozey's Furniture and Appliances and outside to the building where his boat was stored.

Cooper climbed the ladder and sat in the cockpit. Big smile. Then he went down the gangway and into the cabin.

"Wow."

"I'm rebuilding it."

"How long's it going to take?"

"Another six months, maybe."

Six months? From what I could see he hadn't fixed a plank since the first time I saw it.

Rozey led us back to the barn and into his workroom where he had all his stuff lying around on the floor and leaning up against the walls: tools and ladders, old lawn-mowers and a couple of old bikes and chairs, wood-frame windows, a few doors.

"You've got a shitload of stuff," said Cooper.

"You can never have too much stuff," said Rozey. He edged his way through all the stuff to the far side of the room. There were half a dozen fishing rods supported on nails driven into the walls, four fishing nets and, on the floor, a whole bunch of tackle boxes.

"You boys feel like doing a little fishing?"

"Yeah," said Cooper. "I love fishing."

He had a kind of faraway look in his eyes. I was think-ing about him on the front porch with his fishing gear. Waiting for his father who never bothered to show up.

Rozey brought down a couple of fishing rods.

"Pick yourselves a tackle box, boys." We headed down the hill to the meadow that bordered the river at the back of Rozey's property.

"Man, this is beautiful," said Cooper.

"Oh, boy," said Rozey. "It's my favorite place in all the world. You oughta see it first thing in the morning. You can see the stars and the moon. You can hear the fish jumping. Lots of times there are deer right here in the meadow just staring at you, hoping you don't have a gun." He laughed. "One time I come down here in hunting season. Big clutch of cows just over there." He pointed to some trees by the riverbank. "And right in the middle of all the cows was two deers pretending to be cows. Safest place in two counties."

Rozey led us down a path through the meadow to a clearing by the river where there were a couple of old kitchen chairs and a table and, just beyond them, a short wooden dock covered with old carpet. Tied to the dock was a rowboat — white on the outside, varnished on the inside.

"Hop in, boys."

He undid the ropes, tossed them, then stepped into the boat and sat down, pushed us away from the dock with one oar, then put the oars in the oarlocks and rowed us out into the river. Cooper was sitting in the bow and I was in the stern.

Rozey rowed and rowed. Cooper and I just sat there watching the ends of our rods, looking at the river, at the hills that rose up on either side of the valley. The only sounds were the creaking of the oars and the little splash as Rozey dipped them in the water and drew them back.

None of us said a word. None of us had to.

We were out on the river maybe half an hour before Cooper said, "I love this boat, Rozey."

"My dad built it," said Rozey.

"How long's he been dead?" said Cooper.

"Six years."

"You miss him?"

"Oh, boy," he said, "I do miss him. Yes, I do."

I couldn't look at Cooper. I just turned and looked out at the river behind us, watched the end of my fishing rod, waiting.

But it was Cooper who got the first hit. The tip of his rod almost hit the water.

"Whoa!"

It *was* a whoa. Rozey shipped the oars and reached for the net. He had lots of time to get ready. Cooper must've worked the fish for ten minutes before it broke water.

"It's a big sonofabitch," said Cooper. He worked it for another five minutes before he got it in close enough for Rozey to net it.

The pike must've weighed about ten pounds. It thrashed around in the net in the bottom of the boat for a couple of minutes before Rozey could get a grip and break its neck.

"Looks like you just caught us our supper, Cooper."

Cooper kept looking down at that fish and smiling like a madman. It was the happiest I'd ever seen him.

Fifteen minutes later Rozey had the boat tied up and the fish on the dock.

He pulled out his knife and said, "Here, you caught it,

you clean it," and showed Cooper how to do it. Ten minutes after that, we were up in Rozey's kitchen with the fish in the frying pan, Cooper in charge.

"Keep flippin' them till they're done," said Rozey.

"Whoa," said Cooper, when he had his first bite. "I've never tasted fish like this."

"There's nothing like fish out of the river and into the pan."

"You can say that again," said Cooper.

"There's nothing like fish out of the river and into the pan." He laughed, and we laughed, too. When we were done, Cooper got up from the kitchen table and started to clean up the kitchen.

"Leave that," said Rozey. "It'll give me something to do tonight. And I better be gettin' you boys back."

Cooper was pretty quiet the whole way back into town. When Rozey pulled to the curb on the side street near the school, I got out and Cooper just sat there for a minute.

"Thanks, Rozey." He reached out his hand and Rozey shook it.

"No problem, Cooper. Come along any time."

Cooper and I headed up the street and back to school.

"I'm sorry what I said about Rozey. About him being a retard. That was an ignorant thing to say. That was the best day I ever had."

When we climbed the stairs from the front doors and

turned to head down the hall, Cruickshank was still down on his knees scrubbing the floor with what was left of his toothbrush.

Cooper and I sat together at the back of the room for mail call. Docherty was the same old comedian, tossing letters around the room in the general direction of the person who was supposed to get them.

"That's it, boys," he said. Cooper was looking down at his desk as usual.

"Oh, wait," said Docherty, feeling around in the bottom of the bag. He pulled out a final letter. "It seems Mr. Cooper has a letter. Finally."

What a prick. He fired the letter over Cooper's head. Cooper scrambled to retrieve it.

Later, Cooper sat on the low wooden bench in front of his locker. He was staring at the letter, like he was afraid to see what might be in it. Finally he opened the envelope and pulled out the letter and read it. He spent a long time reading it. Then he folded it and put it back in the envelope.

"Home?" I said.

"Hm?" He turned to look at me. There were tears in his eyes.

"A letter from home?"

He turned to face the wall.

5

COOPER WAS GETTING weirder and weirder. Half the time I'd see him coming and he'd turn and head in the other direction. I was still going out to our favorite place every day before classes, freezing my ass off in that Jeezus freezing November wind. No Cooper. I spotted him a couple of times way at the end of the school yard standing by the fence staring up at that hill back of town, the cars and trucks heading out on that highway.

Then all of a sudden, like he'd flipped some kind of brain switch, he'd come up smiling, give me a poke on the shoulder. "What's up, asshole?"

One morning, right before class, a kid named Masterson was kicking a soccer ball. A couple more kicks, Masterson was in shit. The ball went right through the window. Masterson went off to The Dungeon.

A few minutes later, Rozey showed up with a trash can, pair of pliers and work gloves.

"Hey, Rozey."

"Oh, boy." Gave us one of his smiles. "Some mess, eh?" And he set to work pulling the shards of glass from the window frame, dropping them in the trash can. One shard at a time. Pull a shard, drop it in the can. Pull a shard . . .

"At this rate he should be done by Christmas."

Cooper spun on Carruthers. Poked him in the chest. "Fuck off."

"I'm only saying . . ."

"He's doing his best. Leave him alone."

A few minutes later Rozey was done pulling the shards.

"I'm going to go down there and clean up," he said, pointing to the basement room.

"Very good," said Father Bartlett.

Next thing you know, we're looking at Rozey through the window.

"Oh, boy," he said. "It's a real mess down here, Father. Glass all over."

"No shit," said Carruthers. One swift punch in the gut and Cooper left him bending over at the waist, trying to catch his breath.

"Jeezus," said Carruthers. "I was only . . ."

"You were only being an asshole." He gave him a rap in the crotch. "Say one more word, I'll crush your nuts."

In class, Cooper and I still sat at our same desks across

from each other, and we still walked together from class to class, but normally he never had much to say.

"You all right, Cooper?"

"What?"

"You get bad news from home?"

"Home?"

"Your letter."

"Oh, that." He shook his head. "No, nothing like that."

"You want to talk?"

"Not really."

He didn't feel much like talking in class, either. When teachers asked him questions, he'd make like he hadn't heard, like he was daydreaming.

"Mr. Cooper, are you with us?"

"Unfortunately," he'd say. Or, "Sadly, yes."

"If it wouldn't be too inconvenient, Mr. Cooper, perhaps you'd be good enough to get to your feet and answer the question."

"What question was that?"

Strap time for Cooper. And he'd head for the front of the room, hold out his right hand, then his left, staring right at whoever was hammering away. Never flinched. Once, when Sullivan had given him five on each hand, Cooper just looked at him and said, "You done?" Five more.

He didn't seem to want to talk to me or to be with me at school, but on Saturdays Cooper was still my shadow.

From first thing in the morning, through breakfast and study hall, he stayed as close as he could, and when it came time to head for the doors, he was right there. My own seeing-eye Cooper.

"You going to Rozey's?"

"Yeah."

"Can I tag along?"

"Sure."

We went fishing one more time in early November, never mind the cold. We sat on the dock all bundled up in our winter jackets and toques and mitts, eating sandwiches and drinking hot chocolate and smoking our cigarettes and watching our bobbers and not really caring one way or the other if we caught anything. Saturdays with Rozey was the only time Cooper seemed like the old Cooper.

Rozey had all kinds of questions for us.

"What do you want to be when you grow up?" he said.

"I don't want to grow up," said Cooper.

"Like Peter Pan?" I said.

"Yeah," he said. "What I've seen of grownups hasn't been very encouraging." Then he looked at Rozey, who was staring at the end of his fishing rod. "Except for you, Rozey. You're about the only normal grownup I've ever met."

"Thanks. I guess." Rozey laughed. "But say you do grow up. What do you want to do?"

"I dunno. Maybe take care of animals."

"Like a vet?"

"Yeah," he said. "Animals that are hurt or sick. Something like that."

Later we put all the fishing gear back in the barn, then got into the truck — Cooper in the middle, me by the door.

Rozey started the engine and put the truck in gear.

He was just turning onto the road when Cooper said, "What happened to your dad?"

"Got the cancer and died," said Rozey.

"How old was he?"

"Seventy-two."

"You were lucky to have him around a long time," said Cooper.

"Yeah."

No more chatter from Cooper. He just sat and stared straight ahead until Rozey pulled the truck to the side of the road half a block from St. Iggy's. I got out and Cooper slid across and got out and looked at Rozey.

"Thanks," he said. "For everything."

Cooper didn't say anything more until we were nearing the front door of the school. Then he stopped and faced me and said, "What do you think happens to us when we die?"

"I don't know."

"Do you think there's a heaven?"

"I hope so," I said.

The faith that looks through death.

"Yeah," I said. "Something like that."

———

WE SAT AT THE back of study hall, but no mail for Cooper or me. Then the whole herd of us headed for the stairs that led down to the yard.

As we got to the top of the stairs, O'Hara started to go past us. Cooper didn't say a word. Just reached out, put both hands on his back and gave him a shove. Next thing you knew, O'Hara was rolling down the stairs.

Cooper ran down and stood over him.

"One word, fuckup. One word." O'Hara wasn't the swiftest kid in the building, but he knew better than to open his mouth. Cooper gave him a kick in the ribs, then stepped over him and pushed open the door. Went out into the yard, back to his old disappearing self.

Klemski looked at me. I looked at Klemski.

"Jeezus," he said.

Cooper sat with us at supper, but he didn't say two words. Just fiddled with his food, then cleared his tray.

Next time I saw him it was bed time. Next time I saw him after that, he was following Prince out of the darkened dorm toward the stairway.

———

NEXT MORNING, COOPER was a lump under the covers, as usual. Bartlett on duty. Bartlett making a beeline for Cooper's bed. Slapped him on the ass with his yardstick.

"Up, Cooper. Now." Cooper didn't move, didn't make a sound. Bartlett grabbed the edge of the blanket and hauled it off the bed. Then the sheet. Cooper was curled on his side with his back to the priest. Bartlett reached down and grabbed Cooper by the shoulder.

"Get your fucking hands off me."

Holy shit.

"What do ..."

"I'm sick. Leave me alone."

"Get up. Now!" Bartlett's voice echoed around the room. Guys were just standing there, stunned.

Bartlett reached down and grabbed Cooper again, by the arm this time, and started hauling him out of the bed. Cooper got about halfway to his feet and then just let go. Puke all over the front of Bartlett's robe, puke on his shoes, the floor.

"Happy now, you dumb shit?" Cooper was death warmed over. His face was all chalky. His eyes were all red. Puke on his chin, puke on his pajamas. He got up and made for the washroom. Made it about halfway there. Then he was down on his hands and knees, letting go again.

Apart from that, no one made a sound. You could hardly breathe. Cooper got up and got himself into one of the stalls, slammed the door. Started throwing up again. Couldn't have been much left to hurl.

We were all just standing there, stunned. Bartlett looked at us.

"Routines," he said. "Make your beds. Clean up. Make yourselves presentable."

Sounded like Cooper was giving it one last go, then silence in there as well.

Guys started making their beds, stepped around the puke and went into the john, then headed to the locker room to get dressed.

I went to the door of Cooper's stall.

"Cooper?" Knocked on the door. "Let me help you to the — "

"Clemson!" Bartlett was standing in the doorway to the bathroom. "Get dressed."

"He needs help. He needs to — "

"He needs to clean up the mess he's just made."

"Are you kidding me? He's just puked his guts out and you expect him to — "

"Time-out room. Now!"

"Are you fucking kidding me?"

———

IT WAS DUNLOP who let me out of The Dungeon. I was sitting in the corner, starkers. I'd used my pajamas to wipe myself, then cover up the pile of shit. Dunlop kind of reeled back from the smell when he opened the door. Marched me upstairs, watched as I got into new pajamas, then marched me back down to the time-out room and watched as I cleaned up the mess. Marched me back up to the dorm and made me clean up Cooper's mess as well.

"Father Bartlett said if you were so keen to help your friend, this would be the least you could do." Must've been ten-thirty by the time I was all done. I smelled of puke but who cared? I was thinking about Cooper puking all over the front of Bartlett's robe.

"What are you laughing about?"

Dunlop could go right on waiting for an answer.

A day in The Dungeon. A week's worth of detentions, two hours a shot.

Worth every minute of it.

I pulled the covers over my head. Must've fallen asleep within two minutes of putting my head on the pillow.

———

NEXT MORNING, NO Cooper. His bed was just the way he left it — sheets and blankets in a mess — when he went off to the infirmary.

I was in no mood to even look at Bartlett, much less hear him snore on about the Pope.

Five minutes into class, I stuck my hand up.

"Yes, Mr. Clemson."

"Can you explain again about papal infallibility?"

"Papal infallibility means the Pope, as the church's supreme teacher of the faithful, cannot err when he proclaims a doctrine of faith or morals."

"So he can't make a mistake?"

"Not when it comes to these matters," said Bartlett.

"How is that possible?"

"How is what possible?"

"How can it be possible that someone can't make a mistake? We all make mistakes. We're human. Isn't the Pope human?"

"Of course."

"Well, if he's human, he can make mistakes. Right?"

"Not the Holy Father," said The Pear. "Not in these matters."

"But in other matters. Let's say he's out driving."

"The Pope doesn't drive."

"Well, let's say he does. Let's say he's out for a spin and goes through a red light. Wouldn't that be a mistake?"

"Yes," said The Pear. "But we're not talking about running red lights. We're talking about matters of doctrine. In these matters, the Pope is infallible."

"So he can make mistakes, but he's still infallible?"

"Yes." The Pear was about to move on. But I wasn't.

"Another thing," I said. "What's with the get-up the Pope always wears? The big hat, the fancy robes."

"They're a sign of his exalted office."

"You think Christ would be caught dead in a get-up like that?"

Whistles and cheers.

"Pardon?" The Pear came down the aisle until he was standing right beside me. "What did you say, Mr. Clemson?"

"I said Christ wouldn't be caught dead wearing all that crap the Pope wears — robes and rings and that thing on his head. It's all a lot of papal bull."

"On your feet. Now!"

At least it was a different dungeon. And it was only for a couple of hours.

I didn't think things could get any weirder. But it's just when you think something like that that things are bound to get weirder than ever.

I got through the rest of my classes, zipped up to check on Cooper, who still looked half dead, went down, had supper, had a smoke, had a shower and fell asleep in about two seconds flat.

Next thing I knew, Prince was tapping me with his yardstick.

"Come with me," he whispered.

What the fuck? I got up on one elbow and looked at him. All I could see was his outline silhouetted against the red glow of the exit light above the door at the end of the dorm.

"Come with me." He turned and walked away.

I swung my feet out from under the covers and sat on the edge of the bed for a minute, rubbed my eyes and ran my hands through my hair. My heart was pounding.

I turned and looked at Cooper's empty bed. I got up and walked barefoot down the length of the dorm, out the door and down the stairs.

Prince's door was open. There was a weird flickering light. I went in and stood just inside the door. The room was lit by candles. Must have been ten of them here and there on the desk, the bureau, on top of the bookshelves.

"Close the door," he said. He was sitting on a couch against the window wall. I closed the door.

"Come in," he said. He patted the couch. "Sit down."

I crossed the room and sat down, probably right where Cooper usually sat, leaving as much space between us as I could. Prince turned to face me, his back against the far end of the couch, folding one leg under the other. He had his arm on the back of the couch. Mr. Casual.

We just sat there for a minute looking at each other. Then he smiled — one of those sick smiles adults put on when they're trying to be sincere.

"I visited Timothy this afternoon. He told me what happened with Father Bartlett. Afterwards I had a word with Father Bartlett. I told him I wasn't happy with the way he treated Timothy. Or you."

"And?"

"He apologized. He said he let things get a little out of hand. He said it wouldn't happen again."

"Good for him." My heart was still racing. But thinking of Bartlett, the way he'd treated Cooper, made me angry all over again.

One of Prince's eyebrows got a little twitchy, but he didn't say anything and we sat there for a few minutes on either side of a big chilly silence.

"You haven't been happy here, have you?"

"Who could be?"

"Were you angry? When your parents sent you here?"

"My parents didn't send me here. My mother's boyfriend sent me here. And, yeah, I was angry. I'm still angry."

He leaned a little toward me. Got one of those big Mr. Serious looks on his face.

"How were things at home?"

"Shitty."

"Well, you and Timothy both seem to have had a pretty unhappy time of it."

"You can say that again."

"Would you like to talk about it?"

I shook my head. No way I was unloading anything on a guy like him.

"Timothy has been finding it helpful."

"Finding what helpful?"

"Talking. Sharing your thoughts can be a great relief," he said.

I shook my head.

"Would you like something to drink?"

"Drink?"

"Pop? Water?"

Shook my head again. "I'm beat. I just want to get back to bed."

"Certainly. Yes. It's getting late."

He leaned toward me, put his hand on my thigh, gave a little squeeze, looking me right in the eye all the while.

"Come back any time." Another squeeze.

Come back any time? He made it sound like I'd just turned up at his door for a little heart-to-heart.

"If you feel like talking, I would be more than happy to listen. To offer whatever advice I could."

What was I supposed to say to that?

"Good night," he said.

Took me half an hour to get to sleep, trying to figure out what all that was about.

———

BY SATURDAY, COOPER was back from the dead. Didn't look a hundred percent, but wasted no time getting his coat and hat on and heading for the door. Rozey was parked in the usual place. He had the engine running and the heater going. It was freezing, and the first snow was flying.

"Welcome to winter, boys. It'll be snowing from now right through to May."

"Great," said Cooper. "Can hardly wait."

"What do you boys feel like doing today?"

"Rozey?" I said. "Can I ask you a favor?"

"Sure."

"Can Cooper and me be alone at your place for a little while?"

"No problem. I got some things need doing. Got to get to the dump. And I got some things to do in town." Rozey drove us out to the farm.

We watched him head back down the lane. Then Cooper turned and went into the house. We stamped the snow off our boots and hung up our coats.

"What's up?" Cooper dropped his smokes on the kitchen table, grabbed an ashtray from the sideboard, sat down. I sat across from him.

"Prince called me out the other night."

"He told me."

"What did he say?"

"That you and him had a nice little chat." Cooper gave

me a funny look. Then he went to work on one of his fingers.

"It wasn't a chat, exactly." Cooper looked up at me, then back at his finger, started chewing again. I told him all about it, pretty well word for word.

"'A pretty unhappy time of it?'" Cooper looked up at me. "That's what he said?"

I nodded.

He smiled. "He hasn't been listening. Fucking miserable time is more like it." He chewed off a chunk of skin, spat it out. Then he gave up on his finger and lit a smoke.

"You know what I was thinking this morning?" he said.

"What?"

"All the time I was growing up, no one ever hugged me."

"Your mom never hugged you? Your dad?"

"Never."

Who could imagine that? My old man was always giving me pats on the shoulder, putting his hand on the back of my neck, giving me a squeeze. My mom was always fussing with my hair, giving me kisses when I headed out the door. Big hugs every now and then for no reason. Used to, anyway, before Henry showed up.

How weird would it be if no one ever did that?

There was a long pause. Then Cooper said, "Last night I dreamed about my mother. It was sort of like her and sort of not. She was my mother but she didn't look like my mother. I was telling her what was happening to me and she just held me and smoothed my hair and said, 'Don't worry, Timmy, everything will be all right.' She never held me in my whole life, so where's that come from? That's what got me thinking about never being hugged." He was rolling the end of his cigarette against the edge of the ashtray, then stubbed it out. "Nobody ever loved me."

What do you do when someone tells you something like that? I wasn't so sure my mom and dad loved me anymore. But they used to, when I was little. I knew that much. I couldn't imagine what it would be like to say no one had ever loved you, and mean it.

"I used to wonder what it would be like," he said. "You know, to live in a normal family with brothers and sisters, a mom and a dad. Get up in the morning, a whole bunch of us, getting ready for school, having breakfast together, talking and laughing. Come home after school, have supper together, maybe play games or just sit around and read the paper. You know, just normal stuff.

"Every once in a while someone would invite me over to their place after school so I knew some people actually had lives like that. I could hardly stand it, knowing I had to go back to my foster home. And I knew it wouldn't have been any better if I was still at home. My mother always buzzed, all her so-called friends over drinking their brains out. You never knew what was going to happen next but you knew whatever it was, it wasn't going to be good. There was always fights and you'd wake up to the sound of bottles breaking and people screaming and swearing. I'd put my clothes on and just get the hell out of there. There was a little lawn shed out back and I'd just go in there and shut the door and try to sleep until morning.

"It was pathetic, seeing your mother all spaced out, surrounded by all these jerks. And the worst thing was knowing that they meant more to her than I did.

"When the social worker took me home for a visit and said this is no place for you, honey, she was right. What she didn't say was there *was* no place for me. I wasn't very old but I was old enough to know that. And I knew that this woman who hardly knew me cared more about what happened to me than my own mother did. And she was being paid to care."

He started to cry. "Shit," he said.

I was thinking of how me and my dad always sat together on the couch, him reading to me before bed, me snuggling right up against him.

What would it be like if no one ever did that with you?

"You talk with Prince about all this?"

He nodded. "Yeah." Lit up another smoke. Exhaled. "That's how it started, anyway." He looked down at the table, then up at me. "Next thing, he's sliding over beside

me on the sofa, putting his arm around my shoulders."
He shook his head, drew on his cigarette, looked at me.
"First time anyone had ever done that. Ever hugged me."
He looked at the window, shook his head. "Fuck," he said.
"How could I have fallen for that?" He smoked the rest of
his cigarette, then stubbed it out.

"I hate what's happening to me. I hate it that I go with
him and do all those things with him but part of me thinks
I must like it, like he says I do. I can't stand to think that
I do but sometimes I think maybe I do. That's the sickest
thought. And I can't get away from him. I'm in The Dungeon, I'm in class, out in the yard and I'm trying to think
of other things and then he's right there inside my head.
It's like he's taken over my whole life. It's like he's gotten
right inside me. Jeezus." He looked at me. "Don't let him
start with you, Teddy." He shook his head. "Don't let him
start."

We just sat there like that for a couple of minutes, looking at each other.

"You've got to talk to someone. Tell someone."

He looked at me. Sarcastic little grin. "Like who?"

"Stewart. For starters. If he doesn't do something, we
can go to the cops."

"The cops?" He shook his head. "And who do you think
they're going to believe? A thieving little kid, or a priest?"

"They'll have to believe you. I'll go with — "

"Drop it," he said.

"Cooper . . ."

"Drop it." He pushed his chair back from the table. "I gotta take a whiz. Get the cribbage board and the cards."

And that's how Rozey found us — slapping down cards, moving the pegs — when he came back.

————

HE DROPPED US off at the usual spot. We waved and headed up the street.

"Jeezus, it's freezing," said Cooper. He started to run. He was long gone by the time I got inside. I ditched my coat and headed to study hall for mail call. No Cooper. Just as well. No mail for Cooper.

"Clemson?"

I put up my hand.

Docherty whistled a parcel in my direction. I shot up my hands and grabbed it.

"Nice catch," he said.

"Nice throw," I said. "For a change." Even he laughed.

I took the parcel out to the yard, found a spot more or less out of the wind, lit up a smoke and opened the parcel. Cookies, smokes and candies. She'd put her letter underneath everything. I opened the envelope, took out the bills she'd put in there, unfolded her letter.

Dear Teddy,

Haven't heard from you in a while. How about a letter now and then? I wasn't sure what to get you for Christmas so I'm just sending along a few little things. I'm enclosing some money so that you can get yourself something special. Just want you to know that Henry and I are going to Mexico for the Christmas break. I hope you won't mind staying at school over the holidays. I really . . .

I crumpled up the letter and dropped it in the trash can.

6

Most of the boys went home or to relatives' places or somewhere for Christmas. Six of us were left high and dry. Nowhere to go, no one to be with. Cooper and me, of course.

The priests didn't believe in Christmas decorations or Christmas trees. There were no colored lights and no carols. If you didn't know it was Christmas time, you'd never guess by the looks and sounds of St. Iggy's.

What kind of priests didn't pay attention to Christmas? Even Rita went all out: little porcelain Christmas tree on the counter by the cash register, cards strung up along the wall behind the counter, strings of lights around the windows.

How hard was it to do things like that?

It made me kind of homesick remembering all the Christmas stuff back home. Me and my dad going out every year to cut the tree, me and Mom decorating it, all the presents that started to pile up under the tree, the lit-up trees you saw in people's houses as you walked along the sidewalk, all the decorations in the store windows downtown, the cheesy Christmas music playing everywhere.

For two weeks we had St. Iggy's to ourselves. Even most of the priests had gone somewhere for the holidays.

The good thing about it was there was no routine. We could get up when we felt like it, the Catholics could go to chapel if they wanted to. Meals were the same time, same crappy food, and then we had the days to ourselves. We could fool around in the gym or go out and slide around in the snow in the yard. We could walk the few blocks to town. It was almost like having your real life back for a while.

It sure beat being back home with my mother and Henry. I wouldn't have minded being back home with Dad, but it seemed like he was busy with his new life.

Cooper spent most of his time with his pal Wordsworth. He sat there by the hour, chewing what was left of his nails and flipping pages, stopping to read a poem, his lips moving as he read. It was as if he was reading the poems out loud, only we couldn't hear. Every now and then he stopped reading and started writing things in the margins. Then he'd go back to reading.

I came up beside him, took him by surprise.

"Read me a poem, Cooper."

He snapped the book shut.

"Not in the mood." He crossed his arms on his desk and put his head down.

The best part of Christmas was we got to hang around with Rozey pretty well every day. Cooper and I went down to the boiler room every afternoon. Rozey brought the cribbage board to work and he'd set it up on an upturned crate and the three of us would sit around and play for an hour, maybe two.

———

THAT WEEK WENT by in a blur. Cooper and I hung out in the yard, we hung out in study hall. He was like the old Cooper again, friendly, fairly chatty.

One morning we were in study hall, just sitting there reading. Cooper closed Wordsworth and looked at me.

"You ever do it with a girl?"

"Not really."

"What do you mean, 'Not really'?"

"Copped a feel once. What about you?"

"Once," he said.

"All the way?"

"Umhm."

It was with the daughter of some foster parents. She was a couple of years older than him. She'd been making little moves on him for a while and then one afternoon when her parents were out she got him down in the rec room and the next thing you knew, they were out of their clothes and onto the sofa.

"What was it like?"

"Short and sweet," said Cooper. "I came in about two seconds." He laughed. "Which was a good thing, because right after I came out, her mother came in. Caught us right there on the sofa with our asses hanging out. That was it for that foster home." He laughed. Then he looked at me. "So I'm not a total homo."

We had our meals together. Sometimes he even came to the gym and played pickup with the other kids who'd been stranded at St. Iggy's over the holidays.

But bed time was pretty weird. There were just three of us in the junior dorm: Cooper and Zits and me. Prince still showed up at shower time, which was even creepier since he couldn't pretend he wasn't staring.

Same routine at night: the door opening, those creepy shoes creaking and squeaking on the linoleum, the swishing of the robes, the flashlight beaming this way and that until he got to Cooper's bed. Same tap-tap. Same "Come with me."

I didn't want to think about what Prince was doing to Cooper. All I knew was it had to be gross, whatever it was. And it was wrecking Cooper.

And then, wouldn't you know it, Prince picked me again.

I swung my feet out from under the covers and sat on the edge of the bed, rubbed my eyes and ran my hands through my hair. I turned and looked at Cooper's empty bed, the sheet and blanket tossed back.

Where the hell had he got to? I got up and walked barefoot down the length of the dorm, out the door and down the stairs. I was thinking about what Cooper had said.

Don't let him start with you, Teddy. My heart was hammering away.

Prince had left his door open. Same weird flickering light from all the candles.

"Come in, Teddy. Close the door." He was sitting at the same end of the couch. "Sit down." He patted the cushion beside him. I sat at the far end. "How are you doing?"

"Fine."

"Are you still angry?"

"Angry?"

"About being sent here?"

"You could say."

"Would you like to talk about it?"

"Not especially."

"Talking often helps. Timothy finds that it does."

"What are you talking about?" Cooper was a mess. Whatever Prince was doing to him was totally fucking him up.

"What has he told you?"

"He doesn't have to tell me anything. All I have to do is look at him, listen to him."

"We're working things through. Exploring his feelings. He's very angry. Very confused. He's had a very rough life. I'm trying to help him get to the bottom of his feelings of anger and bitterness. Help him to move on, be a happier person. That's all I'm doing."

He reached over and gripped my thigh, a little higher than the last time. Gave me a little squeeze.

"Touch is very important, particularly for those who do not feel loved, who do not feel appreciated." I put my hand on his, tried to move it. There was no moving that hand. Sweet Jeezus. A few seconds later, he let go.

We just sat there for a while. One minute my mind was racing, thinking about making a run for the door. The next minute it was like I was looking at myself sitting on the couch. Like I was there, and not really there.

I was looking past Prince at the flames of the candles flickering away on top of the bookshelf. I looked around the room. There was a bed against one wall and a bureau against the wall at the foot of the bed. There was a door on the far side of the bed opening onto the bathroom. In front of the couch there was a coffee table and against the wall just inside the door there was a desk and another bookshelf.

The windows were closed. The place felt suffocating, like the heat was turned way up.

"Would you like pop?"

"Sure."

Prince leaned forward, pulled open a drawer to get out a couple of coasters. Left the drawer open. He stood up and went into the bathroom.

In the drawer there were a bunch of black-and-white photographs. Photographs of boys. Naked boys, naked boys together. Naked boys doing things to each other that I had never imagined.

Prince came back from the bathroom carrying two glasses. He nudged the drawer shut with his knee, set the glasses on the coaster, sat down.

He was looking right at me. Weird little smile.

I picked up the glass he'd set in front of me. I lifted it up like I was going to take a sip, just to sniff it. See if he put something in it. Couldn't smell anything.

Prince smiled. "It's just pop. Sorry I don't have any ice."

I took a sip. Tasted fine. Took another sip, then put the glass on the table.

"Would you like to talk?"

"About?"

"Whatever you'd like. Your anger, perhaps. Your unhappiness."

"Not especially."

He was really spooking me out. I didn't know where to look. I picked up the glass, took another sip. Looked past Prince at the picture of Jesus he had on the wall. But it was the other pictures I couldn't get out of my mind.

"Has Timothy talked to you about what's been troubling him?"

"Yeah," I said. "We talk quite a bit." I couldn't believe what I was saying. Prince was all ears now. He leaned forward. Put his hand back on my thigh.

"What did he tell you?"

He was rubbing his thumb on my thigh. I looked down at his hand, was thinking I should get his hand off my leg, but wound up just looking at it.

"Does he talk much about his life?"

"Huh?"

I was looking down at his hand, thinking how much it looked like a big hairy spider making its way toward my crotch.

"Does he ever talk to you about me, say what he thinks of me?"

I looked up at him. "He thinks the same thing as all the rest of us."

"What's that?"

"That you're a bastard." I couldn't believe what I just said.

Prince laughed.

"Well," he said. "You're not one to mince your words. You and Timothy have that in common." He moved his hand up my thigh. The spider was on the move. Another squeeze. "Does he ever talk about his experience in sex?"

I took another sip of my drink, went to put it down on the coaster, but had a tough time seeing exactly where the coaster was. I squinted my eyes. Moved the glass toward the table. Prince took it from me, put it down.

"What?"

"I wondered if you and Cooper ever talked about sex. About the things you did before you came here. You know."

Next thing I know, he's got his hand on my crotch. Big warm spider massaging my balls. Big smile. "You know, giving the big boy a workout?" Gave me a squeeze.

I stood up, moved back from the couch. I was sweating like a madman. It came over me all of a sudden.

"I'm not feeling too good. I think maybe I should get back to the dorm."

"Of course," he said. He stood up, came over and put his arm around my waist, walked me to the door, opened it. Slid his hand inside my pajamas, gave me a little rub on the ass. "You must come back. We can talk. I think we can be friends. Like Timothy and I. We have become great friends."

"Sure," I said. I headed for the stairs. It wasn't a straight line. I could feel his eyes drilling into my back. I just made it up the stairs and through the dorm and into the john. Lights out.

Next thing I knew I was on the floor in one of the stalls, covered in barf.

"Fuck, Clemson." Klemski's little round hedgehog face was right above me. "You okay?"

———

"WHERE THE FUCK were you last night?"

Cooper was shoving the eggs around on his plate.

"Basement. Rozey's room."

"Ask me where I was."

I told him everything I could remember, up until I puked and passed out.

"That's all? Copped a feel?"

I nodded.

He shook his head. "Jesus, Teddy. You can't be going down there. That's the way it started with me. The very same. You can't be going down there anymore. You can't let him start on you." He looked right at me. "Promise? Promise me?"

I nodded.

"Say it."

"I promise."

———

ON CHRISTMAS MORNING, Cooper and I were awake before the wake-up call. We made it through the morning routines, had a little breakfast, then pulled on our coats and got out of there as fast as we could.

Rozey was waiting, exhaust like a little cloud at the back of his old Ford. Cooper opened the door.

"Merry Christmas, boys." Rozey was wearing one of those Santa Claus hats, red with white trimming, a long tail with a fuzzy white ball at the end.

"Great hat," said Cooper. "So does that make you Santa?"

"We'll see."

Twenty minutes later, Rozey pulled into his driveway, idled up the hill and parked behind the house. He had the turkey in the oven. He opened the oven door so we could have a look.

"Smells great, Rozey," I said.

"How about setting the table? I've just got to get a couple of things ready."

Cooper and I set the table. Rozey had some special Christmas napkins. We put them under the forks, set out the knives, the plates, salt and pepper shakers. It only took us about three minutes. We could hear Rozey rustling around in the living room.

"All right, boys, come on in."

Rozey was standing in front of the tree.

"Jeezus," said Cooper. There were a few presents under-neath and three stockings hanging from nails beneath the living-room window. On each of them Rozey had pinned a bit of cardboard with our names on them.

"What are you waiting for, boys?"

Santa had filled our stockings with gum and red-and-white striped mints, three packs of cigarettes and two pairs of socks each, a deck of cards, nail clippers, combs, ballpoint pens. Everything wrapped except for the orange down in the toe of each stocking.

"Santa must have been up all night," said Cooper. He was sitting cross-legged on the floor with all his stuff in front of him, wrapping paper in shreds everywhere.

I pointed at Rozey's stocking. "Wonder what he brought you, Rozey?"

"Well, let's see."

Rozey took his stocking down and sat with us on the floor. He started pulling little packages out of his stocking, held them to his ear and shook them, squeezed them.

"Hm? Wonder what this is?" He ripped off the paper. "Shaving cream! Just what I needed."

We all laughed.

Five minutes later we were all bundled up at the top of the hill. Rozey was holding his old toboggan by the rope.

"Hop on, boys."

Cooper and I must have gone up and down that hill forty times over the next couple of hours. We could hardly make it up to the top after our last run.

"I don't know about you guys, but I'm cooked," said Cooper. His cheeks were red from the cold and the snow. "If I go down there one more time I'll have to have a nap at the bottom."

"Well, then," said Rozey, "you boys ever been ice fishin'?"

"No," said Cooper. "But I've seen people doing it out on the bay back home. Looked like they were freezin' their asses off."

"I'll take you out and you'll be so hot you'll have to take your coats off."

"Bullshit, Rozey."

What he didn't mention was he'd built an ice-fishing shack on the ice in the cut, thirty or forty feet off the end of the dock. He had a little woodstove. We weren't there fifteen minutes when we took off our coats.

"No fair," said Cooper. "You never told us you had a hut."

We spent the rest of the afternoon peeled down to our shirts, comfy as bugs in a bed, watching the tips of the poles we had lying around the hole in the ice. We had three lawn chairs and, in the middle, an upturned crate like the one in the boiler room. Every now and then we had to stop and haul in a fish. Rozey took them off the hook and dropped them back into the hole.

"No fish dinner tonight, boys."

We played cribbage, one hand after another. Cooper was winning like mad. He had a whole pile of change on his side of the board.

We played maybe half an hour when Cooper turned to Rozey.

"Can I ask you something personal?"

"Sure."

"How come you never had any kids?"

Rozey looked at Cooper, then down at his cards.

"Well," he said. "First, you have to have a wife, which I never did."

"How come?"

"It's like a fishing story," said Rozey. "About the one who got away." He laughed. Not much of a laugh.

We played another hand. Rozey stood up.

"I bet that old bird is just dying to get out of the oven and on the table. What do you say?"

"I say let's haul ass," said Cooper.

We pulled on our coats and headed for Rozey's house. It was dark as The Dungeon and the wind was whipping down the hill and into our faces.

"Jeezus," said Cooper. "How brutal is this?"

"It'll make the house feel all that much warmer," said Rozey, and we made for the lights winking in the windows at the top of the hill.

"This should be a little bit better than anything you'd get at St. Iggy's." The table was cluttered with plates and bowls: stuffing, sweet potatoes, mixed vegetables, cranberry sauce, the works. Rozey stood up to do the carving.

"What part do you boys like?" Cooper wanted a drumstick. I wanted white meat. Rozey had the other drumstick. We all loaded up with stuffing.

"This is the best Christmas dinner I've ever had," said Cooper. He hadn't even taken a bite.

"Well, dig in, boys."

The food tasted even better than it looked. We were all silent for a few minutes, eating away.

Then Cooper said, "You always have a Christmas dinner like this?"

"Oh, yeah," said Rozey. "Me and my dad would spend Christmas morning in the kitchen getting everything ready. Then we'd go out looking for strays."

"Strays?" said Cooper.

"Old bachelors, widows."

"And orphans?" said Cooper.

"Weren't too many orphans around. Dad, he'd say, 'Roger, we got way too much food for just the two of us, and we've told each other pretty well all the stories we know, so let's go round up someone to come over and entertain us.'" Rozey laughed. "So we'd put the turkey in the oven and then drive around and bring in the strays. Sometimes just one, sometimes two. Once we had four. We'd eat and just talk. People love to talk. Especially people who normally spend their whole days talking to their cats or their dogs. Oh, boy, the stories."

"Tell us one," said Cooper.

"Well," said Rozey. "Just up the road here about a mile and a half there were two bachelor brothers. George and Harold Crosley. They lived with their mother on the old farmstead that their father had farmed and his father had farmed. The smallest little house you can imagine. There's one big back room right across the house and then in the front there's two bedrooms and that's it."

"No bathroom?"

"Nope," said Rozey. "They had an outhouse. No running water, no electricity. The boys shared one bedroom and Mother had the other. The boys slept in the same bed from the time they were this high up until their mother died. They were in their sixties. They went to bed in the same clothes they wore all day. Once a week, they used to take their clothes off and have a bath in the kitchen in a big tub with water heated on the woodstove, their mother scrubbing their backs like they were still six or seven. Anyway, Mother had been dead for six or eight months and one night George

— it was him we had over for dinner, Harold being dead —
George turned to Harold and said, 'Harold, I reckon we
don't have to share a bed anymore, do we?' and Harold said,
'No, George, I don't believe we do,' and George got up and
moved next door into Mother's old bedroom."

"Took them six months to figure out there was a spare
bed?" said Cooper.

"Oh, no. But neither one wanted to hurt the other
guy's feelings by being the first to move." Rozey laughed
and laughed. "Ain't that the best?"

"What I wouldn't give for a brother like that," I said.

"Me, too," said Cooper. "What I wouldn't give for a
brother, period."

"What about you, Teddy? You have a favorite Christmas?"

"When I was eleven," I said, "we went to Florida for
Christmas. We had a little house right on the beach. White
with an orange roof. There were palm trees all around the
patio looking out over the ocean. I'd never seen the ocean
before. Christmas morning we went out to the patio, my
mom and me, and my dad brought our breakfast out on
a tray and we sat there looking at the ocean, eating bacon and eggs and toast. Then we spent the day swimming,
hanging around on the beach."

"You have a turkey dinner?"

"Nope. Dad went out and bought a bucket of chicken.
Chicken and biscuits and corn and beans. And key lime

pie for dessert. It was the last time we were really all happy together. When we got home things started going sour. My parents started fighting. I hid out in my room or went over to friends' places. And then my father started to disappear on us. And then two years ago, he left."

Rozey and Cooper were both holding their knives and forks, but they weren't eating.

"I remember the last night he was in the house. I woke up all of a sudden. There'd been some kind of crashing sound, like breaking glass. I went downstairs. My mother was in the living room crying. I asked her where dad was and she pointed to the kitchen. I went in and turned on the light. The window in the back door was smashed. My father was sitting on the counter with a towel around his hand. The blood had soaked right through. He looked at me and said, 'Turn off the light, Teddy. It'll be better for my hand.' So I shut the light and went over to the counter. I asked him what happened. 'I had a little accident,' he said. 'You go back to bed.' In the morning when I came down he'd already gone off to work." I cut another piece of turkey and started eating. "He never came back."

"Jeez," said Cooper.

"That's a sad story," said Rozey. "Not the first part. The first part was nice, but it's a sad ending."

We all went back to eating.

A minute later Rozey looked at Cooper. "You have a favorite Christmas?"

"This one," said Cooper. He helped himself to more stuffing.

Rozey looked a little startled. "Well, say."

We finished our meals. Cooper and me cleared the table, started doing the dishes.

"Leave that, boys. I'll do it later. Time to get into the presents." We made our way into the living room. Rozey leaned down and picked up two parcels from beneath the tree, handed one to Cooper, the other to me. We tore away the wrappings.

He'd bought me *The Old Man and the Sea* by Ernest Hemingway; *The Collected Works of Samuel Taylor Coleridge* for Cooper. "Hazel down at the library helped me pick them out. They ain't new, they're from the used-book bin. But they're in pretty good shape."

Cooper looked at the book and then at Rozey.

"I feel so bad, Rozey. We didn't bring you anything."

"Spending the day with you is all the present I need." Rozey looked at his watch. "I ought to be getting you back."

Twenty minutes later we were standing on the sidewalk, thanking Rozey again and again. Then Cooper slammed the door of the pickup and we waved and headed toward the school, rounded the corner and walked up the drive. Cooper pulled open the front door.

"Shades of the prison-house begin to close / Upon the growing boy..."

"Wordsworth?"

"Of course."

We went up to the locker room and put our presents away, then took a pass on supper and headed to the boiler room. We hunkered down on the floor and had a cigarette.

When I looked over at Cooper, he had tears in his eyes.

"How come you're so sad?"

"I'm not sad, you idiot. I've never been so happy in my life. That was the best Christmas I've ever had. That was the sweetest thing anyone ever did for me, and he's almost a complete stranger." He took off his glasses, wiped his eyes with the palms of his hands.

"What I want to know is, where's he been all my life? How come I got to be fourteen before someone actually went out of his way to do things for me? Take me fishing, take me tobogganing, cook up the best Christmas dinner in the history of the world, sit and talk, sit and listen. What I wouldn't give to be his son. I could've been a great son if I'd ever had the chance." He was biting his lower lip. "Instead, roll of the dice and they came up snake eyes." He lit up another smoke. "Shit."

7

You know how sometimes you wake up in a cold sweat thinking of something awful you did or said, something you can't go back and fix, no matter how bad you wish you could? Well, one morning there I was, wide awake, my palms and forehead all sweaty. Heart racing.

What woke me up was the face of Alan Christie, the kid I'd told Cooper about when he asked me about the worst thing I'd ever done. Christie's nose and mouth bloody from where I'd punched him, tears streaming, dark brown eyes staring up at me like big question marks. He was flat on his back on the grass at the back of my old school. I was standing over him, one foot on either side of his scrawny little chest. I felt like picking him up by the scruff of the neck and hammering him a couple more times. Little prick.

"You say another word about my old man, I'll break your fucking neck." I left him there, all bloody and snotty, wondering what hit him. I could still hear his voice as I walked away: "I'm sorry, Teddy."

This was a couple of weeks after my old man did his disappearing act. It was lunch hour. I was hanging around with Billy Bedford, my absolute best pal, and then Christie came weaseling up. I never did like him. He had a way of trying to get under your skin with little comments. He'd never just come right out and say something. It was like he was talking sideways. Anyway, he comes up and looks at me and he has this little smirk on his face. "See your old man has a new girlfriend. Looks like she's young enough to be your — "

He never got the last word out of his mouth. By that time he was on the ground, bloody and blubbering. I just left him there. I was so mad I couldn't see straight.

I was about a block and a half from the school before Bedford caught up with me, all winded from running. I just kept walking as fast as I could. I was still so pissed.

Finally Bedford grabbed me by the sleeve and we stopped and stood there on the sidewalk staring at each other.

"What's with you, Teddy?"

"You hear what that little shit said to me?"

"Who gives a shit? He's a little weasel. No one pays any attention to him. And besides, he's about half your size. What's going on with you?"

Who the hell knew? All I knew was that I was angry all the time. I felt like I wanted to shove my fist right through things, like my dad did the night he took off.

I didn't care about any of the things I used to care about. My grades were in the toilet. I stopped hanging out with my friends. I spent a lot of time riding my bike down around the harbor or along the river. Sometimes Bedford came looking for me. But eventually he just sort of gave up.

"What's with you?"

Jeezus. Cooper caught me completely by surprise. I was out in the alcove having a smoke, but in my head I was still on that sidewalk back home, Bedford giving me shit.

"Daydreaming," I said.

He hunkered down beside me, lit up a smoke. "What about?"

"Just thinking of a pal of mine back home." I told him about Billy, his goofy knock-knock jokes, the time he put a lizard in the girls' dressing room in the gym. Stuff like that.

"You miss home?"

"Depends." Sometimes I did. I'd get to thinking about the friends I used to have, the fun we used to have goofing around. I even missed my old school, weird as that was. It was hard thinking of the way things had turned out by the time I left town, how I'd become kind of a loner.

But thinking about that made me feel sad, and feeling sad shows on your face faster than a crop of zits. There was nothing the priests and kids like O'Hara couldn't read on your face and you didn't want to give them the edge, that's for sure. Besides, there was no way I could go back and undo what I'd done to Christie. No way I could go back and make up with Bedford. That was all history.

"At least you got a home to miss." He spiraled his cigarette out into the yard, looked at me. "What's your home like?"

"My former home?"

He laughed. "Yeah, that one."

"Nice. Up on a hill overlooking the bay."

"Big?"

"Big enough. Two stories. Four bedrooms."

"What's your old man do?"

"Builds houses. He built that one."

"You go with him? When he's building?"

"Sometimes."

"He let you help?"

"Drive some nails. Hand him his tools. Things like that."

"Was it fun?"

Mostly it was fun just being with him. Watching him do things that he could do really well, working with guys who seemed to like him a lot. Made me feel proud.

"Yeah," I said. "It was."

Cooper didn't say anything for a few minutes. "The letters you get, who sends them?"

"My mother."

"She miss you?"

A year ago I would have said yes. Now? "Your guess is as good as mine. Once her boyfriend moved in, it was like I went out with the trash."

He looked at me, then away. "What about your dad?"

"What about him?"

"He ever write?"

"Nope."

"How come?"

"Beats me."

"He know where you are?"

"I guess."

"Go figure, eh?"

What made it all so weird was, me and my dad used to be so close. He was always interested in what was going on in my life. I'd tell him what I'd learned in school, what me and my friends were up to. He'd laugh in all the right places. Always made me feel that what I did and what I thought really mattered.

How could someone go from caring so much to not caring at all? Made you wonder if it was all bogus from day one.

I looked at Cooper. He was staring down at the ground. "If you ever saw your old man," he said, "what would you say to him?"

"I'd like to tell him what an asshole he was. But I don't know. You?"

"I don't know, either."

I looked over at him.

"You finally got a letter from your mom?"

He didn't say anything for quite a while. Then he said, almost a whisper, "I wrote it myself." He had his hands jammed in his coat pockets, his shoulders hunched up, collar pulled up around either side of his face. The wind was brutal.

"What?"

"I couldn't stand seeing all the other guys getting letters and never hearing my name called out. It was pathetic."

"But you were crying when you read it."

He stood there for a couple of minutes, staring out at the yard.

"I'll tell you this much. No one's gonna miss me when I'm gone." Cooper pushed himself away from the wall and walked away.

Second time he'd said that.

———

THE DAY STARTED out all right. I didn't get centered out in geography, math or history and actually found it sort of interesting talking about what things were like out on the prairies, all the wheat they grew out there, things like that. I was in a pretty good mood. Didn't last.

The worst thing about English was it was the last class before lunch. You could hear stomachs growling up and down the aisles. We were all thinking more about sandwiches and cookies than *Oliver Twist*.

"Mr. Clemson." Sullivan had wandered down our row and stopped right beside me. Must have seen an X on my forehead, got it in his crosshairs.

"Yes," I said.

"Yes, Father?"

"Yes, Father."

"Refresh my memory, Mr. Clemson. You have read *Oliver Twist*, have you not?"

"Yes."

"Yes, Father?"

"Yes, Father."

"Well, in that case, you'll have no trouble telling us all about some of the major characters. Jack Dawkins, for example."

"Yes. Yes, Father."

"Very well, the classroom is yours. Please step up to the front of the room and share the benefits of your wisdom."

I went to the front. Sullivan had gone to the back. He was leaning against the wall. Smirking.

"Jack was one of Fagin's little criminals."

"Which one?"

"Kind of the head little criminal."

"His nickname?"

"The Artful Dodger. It was the Dodger who recruited Oliver into the gang, who brought him to Fagin's place."

"How would you describe Fagin?" said Sullivan.

"He was kind of like a father to all the boys, Father."

"A father?"

"Yes," I said. "Father."

"How would you describe a father?"

"Well," I said, "fathers are supposed to take care of their kids, make sure they get food and clothing, make sure they're okay, spend time with them, have fun with them."

"And would you say that Fagin fulfills all these responsibilities of fatherhood?"

"Better than my old man," I said. There were snickers and snorts up and down the room.

"That'll be enough!" Sullivan glared at the room. Silence.

I started heading for my desk.

"Not you," said Sullivan. "Back to Fagin. Exactly what does he do for the boys?"

"He gives them a place to stay. Feeds them. They have fun together. They're kind of like a big family."

"And what does he train them to do?"

"Pick pockets."

"Do you think he's an admirable person?"

"He's about the only one who's ever cared for any of those kids."

"He cares so much that he turns them into criminals?"

"Yes."

"Father."

"Yes, Father."

"And would you say that's a good thing?"

"He taught them how to make a living. They've got to do something to earn money. At least they're having fun. Better than being in an orphanage. Nobody in any of those places ever gave two sh . . . ever cared what happened to them."

"Do you think that's true of all institutions, Mr. Clemson?"

"Probably."

"This institution?"

"Probably."

"Probably?" I could tell he was getting pissed.

"I wouldn't describe some of the stuff that happens here as caring for someone."

Sullivan pushed himself away from the wall, headed up the aisle toward me.

"And just what do you mean to insinuate by that remark, Mr. Clemson?"

"The way some of the priests treat the kids."

"Would you care to offer an example?"

He was standing about three inches away from me. His breath smelled of mints.

"Sure." I was staring right at him. "When a priest locks a kid in the time-out room and leaves him there so long the kid goes crazy. Or when a priest tells a kid to stand and face the wall and then comes up behind him and slams his face into — "

Sullivan slapped me so hard across the face that I went reeling, hit my head against his desk, wound up on the floor. Then he had me by the ear and was marching me out the door. He shoved me into the time-out room. I hit the chair, hit the floor, hit the wall. He slammed the door.

"This is exactly what I was talking about, you crazy old bastard."

The door opened. Sullivan filled up the doorway. He came into The Dungeon, stood right over me, then leaned down and punched me square in the face.

My head bounced off the wall. Lights out.

It was after nine that night when the light went on. It was Prince, looking a little stunned. He had one look at me and said, "My God." He helped me to my feet, and then lifted me up and started carrying me.

I was a mess. All shit, snot, blood and urine.

"It's all right," said Prince. "It's all right." Never heard that tone of voice before — kind and worried.

He carried me down the hall and up the stairs to the infirmary. Helped me out of my clothes, left them in a pile on the floor, helped me into the shower. I got out of the shower, dried off, wrapped a towel around myself.

"Sit here on the edge of the bed. I'll take care of your clothes and get you some pajamas."

A few minutes later he was back, steadied me as I got into my pajamas and into bed.

"I'll have someone come and look in on you." He started walking toward the door, but turned when he was about halfway there. Looked like he was about to say something. But then he changed his mind.

I was half asleep when he came back with Father Stewart. They hovered over my bed.

"I've called a doctor," said Stewart. "He should be here shortly."

"Thanks," I said.

"I'm not sure what you did to provoke him," said Stewart, "but what Father Sullivan did was not acceptable and I want you to know I'm taking care of it."

I looked up at him. He didn't say anything more, just gave a little shake of his head, and then he and Prince left. I could hear them talking out in the hall. Prince wasn't raising his voice, but I could feel his anger right through the door.

Next thing I knew this skinny old guy, bald with a frizz of white hair, was sitting on the edge of my bed.

"I'm Dr. Harrison. What happened to you?"

I told him everything I could remember from the classroom until the lights went out in the time-out room.

"I just want to check you over." He started with my face, went to touch my nose and I jerked my head back.

"It's all right," he said. "I'll be gentle."

Gentle or not, I just about passed out when he touched my nose.

"Sorry," he said. "Where else does it hurt?"

"Just about everywhere. My head, especially, and my shoulder. I hit my head on his desk when he knocked me down. Here." I touched the right side of my head behind my ear.

He got a little flashlight out of his doctor's bag, gave my head the once-over.

"Let's have a look at that shoulder." I sat up and took off my pajama top. He felt around a little bit until he hit the spot. I winced. "Right there?"

"Yeah."

He had me move my arm up and down.

"Rotate your shoulder for me." I tried, but it brought tears to my eyes. He looked me up and down.

"A lot of bruising," he said. "Does it hurt anywhere else?"

"That's it, mainly."

He helped me get my arms into my pajama top.

"Your nose is broken. But I guess you already knew that." He smiled. "I'm going to put a splint on your nose, tape it up so it will start to heal. You've got some cuts and abrasions on your head but you won't need any stitches. That shoulder may be dislocated, but it could also just be bruising. Let's see how it feels in the morning."

My stomach growled.

"I'll order you something to eat. Then I'm going to give you something for the pain, and something to help you get to sleep."

He rummaged around in his doctor's bag, pulled out a couple of pill bottles, opened them, tapped some pills into his palm.

"Here," he said. "After you've eaten, take both these pills. Next thing you know, you won't know a thing."

Apparently when the doctor spoke, people jumped. Brother Joseph arrived with a tray of food about fifteen minutes later, pulled up the little bedside table, set the tray down. He was trying not to stare, but he was staring anyway.

"My," he said.

"Hi, Bro."

He shook his head. You could tell that just looking at me upset him. He finally looked away, started fiddling with the food.

"I've brought you some chicken soup. I hope it's still hot."

"If it is, it'll be a first." I laughed. Winced.

"Yes," he said. "Well . . . here. Try it."

He stood there while I finished the soup, then took the bowl and handed me a plate with a sandwich.

"Peanut butter and jam. I hope that's all right."

I took a bite. "More than all right, Bro." I finished the half in three bites, took it a little more slowly on the second half. He took the plate and handed me another loaded with cookies. He held out a glass of milk.

"The doctor says to remind you to take your pills." I swallowed them both at once, then finished off the cookies.

"Thanks a million, Bro. That was great."

"If you need anything, I'll be sitting just over there."

"Thanks."

He crossed the room, shut out the overhead light. He sat in an armchair in the corner, a little halo of light over his head from a reading lamp. He picked up a Bible from the table beside the chair and started reading. He probably hadn't finished two pages before he started snoring.

I went to the washroom, looked at myself in the mirror.

Both my eyes were black and blue, my nose was swollen and crusty with blood. I leaned in for a closer look. Definitely not pretty. I raised my right arm about shoulder height, rotated it. It was stiff, but other than that it worked okay. I raised my pajama top. Bruises and scrapes, but nothing major. I felt the back of my head where it had hit Sullivan's desk. I could feel the welt, crusty with blood.

When I came back out, Cooper was standing by my bed. He took one look at me.

"Holy fuck," he said.

"Yeah." I tried a smile. Even that hurt.

"What's with this fucking place, anyway?" said Cooper.

I was about to say something when Brother Joe stirred, looked like he was about to wake up. Then he went back to snoring.

"Gotta go," said Cooper. "Just wanted to make sure you were alive."

"Thanks," I said.

"See you around," he said. Gave me that Cooper smile and then he was gone.

I pulled the covers up and must have been asleep in two seconds flat. When I woke up Joe was gone. Went to the john, my face looked worse than before if that was possible, came back out and there was Bro holding a tray.

"I didn't know exactly what you like for breakfast, so I just brought some of everything."

He set the tray down on the table, then shoved a couple of pillows behind my back so that I could sit up leaning against the end of the bed. They had one of those tables on wheels that you could roll right over the bed so you could sit up and eat.

He'd brought a bowl of cereal, a glass of orange juice,

a plate of bacon and eggs and toast, a couple of slices of French toast, two pancakes, syrup, the works. Nothing like the crap we got in the cafeteria.

"Just eat what you feel like." He dragged a chair from across the room and sat down and watched me go at it. I started with the bacon and eggs and toast, finished off the French toast and pancakes. Drank the orange juice and ate the cereal.

The more I ate, the more he smiled.

"Doesn't seem to be anything wrong with your appetite." He looked at me with a sad little smile. "I can't tell you how sorry I am that this happened. Father Sullivan, he's . . ."

"A bastard," I said.

"He's a very troubled soul. I'm not making apologies for him. But he's been troubled for a very long time. There won't be any more situations. He's been removed."

"Removed?"

"Sent away."

"Where to?"

"I'm not sure. They didn't say. They just told us that the bishop ordered him removed. He left last night. Someone came and took him away in a car. To the city, I think. So you won't be troubled by him again."

"What about Prince? What are they going to do about him?

Brother Joe looked at me in a weird kind of way, tilted his head a little to the side like he hadn't heard exactly what I'd said.

"You know what he's been doing to Cooper?"

"Father Prince . . . he's very close with . . . it was the bishop who sent him last summer." He shook his head. "It's not our place to criticize authority. The priests are in charge here and we are forbidden from criticizing their actions. Just as they are forbidden from criticizing their superiors."

Jeezus, Bro.

———

THREE DAYS IN the infirmary seemed like three weeks. Just me and the clock on the wall ticking the minutes away. I couldn't believe how good it felt to get out of there and actually go back to classes.

"Jeezus," said Klemski when he got his first look at me. "You look like shit."

The other guys didn't say much, but they all had to get a look at me. My eyes were more purple than black, but my nose was still taped up. I looked like I'd been in a car wreck.

The teachers looked, then looked away.

"Wish I had a fucking camera," said Cooper. We were out in the alcove. I'd just lit up, tossed my match.

"I talked to Brother Joe," I said.

"About what?"

"About Prince."

"You did like fuck."

"I did. When he came to see me in the infirmary. After he told me Sullivan was sent away, I asked him what they're going to do about Prince. After what he's been doing to you."

Cooper dropped his smoke. Ground it out with his shoe.

"You fucking prick. Why don't you mind your own fucking business?"

He stalked off, left me standing there.

8

Cooper was doing his disappearing act, giving me a wide berth. Breakfast, he grabbed some toast, then headed out the door. Who knew where?

"What's up with Cooper?" Klemski asked. "He's even weirder than usual these days."

"Lot of stuff on his mind," I said.

I grabbed my tray, made for the counter, then the door.

I sort of snoozed through geography and math. Next up, history. So much for snoozing.

"Mr. Clemson. Would you be so kind as to describe some of the ways — two or three examples will suffice — in which American culture and politics have influenced Canada since World War One." Docherty could be a dink during mail call, but I kind of liked him. Get him in the right mood, and he was fun.

"We get their magazines," I said.

"Have you read any of those magazines?"

"Yeah."

"You mean, Yes, Father?"

"Yes, Father."

"Which magazine springs to mind?"

"*Life. Time.* Things like that."

"And how do you think those magazines might influence people here in Canada?" Docherty was pacing back and forth at the front of the room as he talked.

"Well . . ." *Give me a minute here, Father.* "I think they're mostly writing about American things. American politicians and movie stars. So if Canadians read a lot of that, then they'll start to think like Americans."

"I see," said Docherty. "And could you name an American politician who might have been profiled in *Life* magazine. Or in *Time*?"

"Certainly. President Eisenhower."

"Does he have a first name?"

"Yes, he does."

Cheers and whistles.

"Would you care to divulge it, for those of your classmates who may have missed the last few years or so of current events?"

"Certainly. Dwight D."

"And for another round of applause, Mr. Clemson, can you tell us what the initial D. stands for?"

"I think so."

He extended an up-raised palm in my direction. "Whenever you're ready."

"David."

Docherty led the applause.

"And does President Eisenhower have a nickname?"

"Yes."

"Don't keep us in suspense, Mr. Clemson."

"Ike."

"Bravo, Mr. Clemson. You are a wizard of history. We'll have a medal struck in your honor. You may take your seat."

———

"WHAT'S WITH DOCHERTY?" said Klemski. We were on our way to English.

"Beats me," I said.

"Never seen him in that kind of good mood before."

"Me, either."

"Too bad they aren't all like Docherty," said Cooper. Where the hell had he come from? "This place wouldn't be such a hellhole."

"Ever wonder why they're such bad-tempered old men?" said Klemski.

"You'd be bad tempered if you had to swear off women and booze and poker and they made you walk around in wool robes all the time," I said. "Makes you wonder why they signed up in the first place."

"My mom says a lot of them signed up when they were kids. Seventeen, eighteen," said Klemski. "Before they knew any better. And it was a big deal to have a priest in the family."

"If they're so miserable all the time, why don't they just quit?"

"What would they do?"

"Painting barns would be better than this," I said.

The best thing about Sullivan getting the big hook, apart from the fact he wouldn't be beating the shit out of me or anyone else, was that Bro Joe took over his English class. Bye-bye Oliver. Bro Joe said we could talk about any books we wanted.

"What do you boys like to read?" A couple of guys said they liked detective books. Someone said they liked cowboy stories. "What about you, Teddy?"

I told him I'd just finished *The Old Man and the Sea*.

"What do you think it's about?" he said.

I said it was about an old man looking for the big catch of his life.

"And why would an old man be so determined to land the fish of his life?"

"He wanted to show everyone that he still could. That he was still a fisherman."

"And why was that important?"

"Because they were all laughing at him. Making fun of him. They all thought he was washed up."

"And why would that matter to him?"

"He was proud," I said. "He was the best once and he wanted to prove that he hadn't lost it just because he was old."

"He was indeed a proud man," said Bro Joe. "Proud and brave and determined not to be defeated. Do you remember that wonderful line? 'A man can be destroyed but not defeated'? What do you think Hemingway meant by that?"

Klemski's hand shot up.

"Something to do with dying? Maybe he meant that the old man had to die, but he didn't have to die a beaten man."

"Very good, Walter."

Walter? He was beaming a big smile at Bro Joe.

I put up my hand.

"Yes, Teddy."

"Maybe the old man knew that he was going to die, but he wanted to die his way, to be a fisherman right to the end. Maybe his fight with the fish was the way he wanted to go out, to be remembered. Not for catching the big fish necessarily, but for going after it and fighting it even if in the end he lost it to the sharks. He'd still made his point."

"Which was?"

"To show them what kind of man he was. Now that he caught his fish he can die a proud man. He can go out on his own terms. Maybe that's the main point."

Brother Joe looked at me. He nodded. "Maybe that is the main point," he said. "To live your life on your own terms, right to the end. Perhaps it's the fight that matters, not the prize."

"So you can die and still win?"

"Yes," said Bro Joe. "We're all going to die. That's not what's important. What's important is how we live."

Lunch was the usual crap. Noodles with cheese slathered all over it. They'd been left out so long the cheese had gone all crusty and wrinkly. Disgusting. I gave that the pass. Peanut butter and jam sandwiches. Hard to screw that up. I took two. Glass of milk. Handful of potato chips. A couple of cookies.

Brother Wilbur was standing guard at the end of the line. What a dink. He gave our trays the once-over as we passed him on our way to our table.

Cooper was ahead of us in line, took his tray and headed for a table at the far side of the room, sat at the end facing the wall, reading Wordsworth, scribbling stuff in the margins and eating at the same time.

"What's with him?" said Henderson.

"Leave him alone," I said.

Anderson was lifting the top piece of bread to see what

the kitchen goofs had done to his peanut butter and jam.

"What are all these little lumps?"

"Peanuts, by chance?" said Klemski.

"They don't look like peanuts."

"What do they look like?" Klemski lifted the top piece off his sandwich.

"I dunno," said Anderson. "Maybe some kind of pills."

Laughter all around the table.

"Laugh all you want. But those guys are putting something in our food. I'm tellin' you."

I wolfed down my last sandwich and stood up.

"What's your hurry?"

"Got to get out of here before Anderson comes down with the Bubonic Plague. Or Hatfield comes out with another of his jokes."

I'd just about had it with both those guys. Anderson and all his nutty talk about food, Hatfield and his jokes. I was feeling like the walls were closing in on me.

Klemski kept on eating. "Can I have your chips?"

"Be my guest." I dumped the chips from my plate onto his. "See you in class."

———

"Hi, Rozey."

"Hey, Teddy."

Rozey was sitting on his chrome-legged chair eating a sandwich. His metal lunchbox was on the floor beside him, top open, the Thermos sitting beside it.

"If I knew you were coming, I'd have made two sandwiches. Want a cookie?"

"Sure."

I opened up the wax paper and took a cookie, handed him the rest.

"No. Help yourself. I got lots more at home."

I got my wooden box, set it on its end and sat down. The cookie was great. I had another. I was thinking about Cooper asking Rozey why he didn't have kids and about Rozey's answer about the one who got away.

"Rozey, you ever have a girlfriend? A real one, not an air freshener."

He chewed on his sandwich and swallowed and looked at me.

"Oh, yeah," he said. "I had a girlfriend one time."

"How come you never got married?"

He shook his head. "Turned me down."

"What was her name?"

"Lucy."

He leaned to his left and pulled the wallet from his back pocket, opened it up and pulled out a black-and-white snapshot.

Lucy was a looker. Big cloud of black hair, dark eyes,

a smile that would keep you awake at night. It was like she was thinking about something, or about someone, and couldn't help but smile. Her eyes were smiling, too.

"Wow."

"Yeah," said Rozey. "Me and her went to grade school together. When I came back from the woods, she was finished school, working in her father's store. They own the hardware."

"She still in town?"

"Yup. Married, three kids. Two boys and a girl." He shook his head. Had a sad little smile on his face. I handed him the picture. He slipped it into its spot, then opened the change pocket of the wallet and pulled out a ring. "Should've bought her a bigger one, I guess." He handed me the ring: gold with a shiny little diamond.

"You gave her this?"

"Tried to," said Rozey. He laughed and put the ring back in his wallet. "Took her out for a fancy dinner at the hotel. When we were done eating, we ordered pie and ice cream. While we were waiting I said, 'Lucy, would you marry me?' She got tears in her eyes. I thought for sure she was going to say yes, but she handed the ring back and got up from the table and ran out of the room."

Rozey's eyes welled. He pulled a handkerchief from his back pocket.

"What'd you do?"

"I put the ring back in my wallet, had my pie and ice cream and went home." He laughed. "I woulda ate hers, too, but I was too full from the steak."

"You never asked her again?"

"Nope," he said.

"You still see her around?"

"Oh, yeah. She's took over her old man's store. You go in there, it'll be Lucy behind the counter."

"Isn't it kind of weird? Running into her?"

"The first couple of times. But we're kind of pals now. We say hi and smile at each other."

"That's the saddest story."

"My old man, he told me, your heart's gotta get broke at least once for it to work right. So mine's workin' just fine now."

———

I COULDN'T GET Rozey's story out of my head. All during religious studies while Bartlett blathered on I was picturing Rozey and Lucy in that hotel dining room — Rozey all sweaty and nervous, Lucy with no clue what was going on in Rozey's head. I could see Rozey bringing out the ring and Lucy running out of the room. I saw all the heads turn to look at her and then turn back to look at Rozey sitting there having his pie and ice cream all by himself.

Brother Julius wanted us to do pencil sketches.

"You can do a still life. You can draw what you see out the window. You can sketch your neighbor, or sketch from memory."

That was easy. I could see Lucy's face as clearly as if I had Rozey's little black-and-white snapshot in front of me.

I drew her looking down so that you saw her big halo of hair and then her forehead. Her eyes looked like they were shut. I tried drawing tears, but they didn't seem right, somehow, so I rubbed them out. I drew her nose and her chin.

But it was her mouth that stumped me. I wanted to draw her lips so they would look like the lips of someone who knew she had just made the biggest mistake of her life.

I drew and erased and drew and erased. Finally I left the face blank where the mouth would be.

"She looks very sad," said Brother Julius.

"Yes," I said. "She's just broken someone's heart."

"Seems she broke her own as well."

"I can't seem to get the mouth right."

"I'm not surprised," he said. "The entire drawing will be in those lips. That's why you've left them until the last. You'll need to think about them. Leave it for now and come back to it."

———

END OF THE day, I was out in the alcove. Jeezus freezing January. Wind, snow, the works. Cooper rounded the corner, collar turned up. Lit a smoke, put his back to the wall, just stood there for a few minutes.

"Sorry," he said. "About the other day."

"No problem," I said. "I didn't mean to go behind your back, Cooper. It's just that Joe showed up, told me they'd gotten rid of Sullivan and I said — "

"It's all right," he said. "Everybody knows anyway."

He was looking across the yard at the hill, the trucks and cars heading west.

"I used to dream about getting on a boat, one of those ocean freighters, maybe get a job as a cabin boy or something and work my way around the world. I'd look at the atlas and pick places I wanted to see: Shanghai, Hong Kong, Istanbul, Athens, Rome, London. All those places sounded so great to me. I could picture myself getting off the boat and just wandering around. I convinced myself I really could do it some day. I had no idea."

"About what?"

"That it would never happen."

"What do you mean? You're fourteen. You've got your whole life ahead of you." I pointed to the road that snaked up the hills and out of town. "All we've got to do is go up there and stick out our thumbs."

He shook his head. "I can't."

"What are you talking about?"

"Prince told me if I leave, it'll be considered escape custody. The courts sent me here and if I run away it'll be like escaping from jail. He said they'll haul me back into court and sentence me to juvenile. And instead of six months, it would be a year, maybe more. I couldn't take that," he said. "But the thing is, I can't take this, either."

We stood there for a few minutes without saying anything. Finished our smokes. Lit up again. Stood there staring at the tail lights disappearing over the crest of the hill.

"Prince says what's been happening, he says I like it as much as he does. Sometimes I think maybe I do. Maybe I am a homo. Maybe I just didn't know it. He says if I tell anyone about anything, he'll tell them that I started it. That I asked for it. I dunno. I just don't know anymore. I think I'm going crazy. Fuck." He wiped his eyes with the palms of his hands, turned and walked away.

———

It was Prince, as usual, who supervised the showers and watched as we dried off and got into our pajamas. Prince who shut off the light and closed the door. Prince who came back half an hour later and went right to Cooper's bed. Prince who leaned over and whispered, "Come with me."

I wanted to tell him to leave Cooper alone. I wanted to jump on him and just start whaling away with my fists. I wanted to kill him.

But all I did was watch him go, watch Cooper follow along a moment later.

I tried to stay awake until Cooper came back, but I couldn't. When I finally woke up, it was still dark. The only sound I could hear was the guys breathing. Cooper's bed was empty.

I headed for the washroom. I could see Cooper's feet in the last stall. His feet seemed to be in shadows or something. Weird. I took another few steps, leaned half over to get a better look under the door.

It wasn't shadows. Cooper's feet were in a puddle of blood.

"Cooper?"

He said something, but it was so faint I couldn't make it out. I got down on the floor, crawled under the door and into the stall. Cooper was leaning back against the tank, an arm on either leg, palms up. He'd wrapped both forearms in towels and the towels were soaked right through.

"What the fuck have you done, Cooper?"

He could only manage to half open his eyes. He held out his hand.

"Take this," he said. "Keep it." He handed me his switchblade. He'd wiped it off and folded the blade.

"I'm going for help."

"No," he said. "Stay with me. Put the knife in your pocket."

I put it in the pocket of my pajama top.

"I can't just let you die, Cooper."

"I'll hate you forever if you don't." He closed his eyes. "Hold my hands," he said.

He closed his eyes and held my hands. A couple of moments later, his hands went limp. His head slumped to one side.

I just stood there staring at him. I leaned down and took his face in my hands. He'd gone all gray. I rubbed his eyelids with my thumbs, but they didn't open.

"Cooper?"

I unlocked the door to the stall and ran through the dorm and down the stairs. I went straight to Prince's door and started pounding on it with my fists.

"Prince, you bastard!"

Prince came out of his room, wrapping his bathrobe around himself, tying the belt.

"What's the meaning of this?"

Then he had a look at my face. He looked at the blood on my hands, on my pajamas.

Prince's face went white. It was like someone punched him. He was trying to say something, but he couldn't get his breath.

"Upstairs," I said. "In the washroom." I ran down the hall and up the stairs and Prince was right behind me taking the stairs two at a time. By the time we got to the washroom, the entire dorm was awake and there was a crowd outside Cooper's stall.

"Get the fuck out of here!" Prince screamed it, the veins in his neck bulging. "All of you. Now!"

Then all hell broke loose. More priests arrived and we were all herded down the stairs and into the study hall. Then we heard the sirens, all kinds of hollering in the hallways, footsteps on the stairs. Things seemed to quiet down until we heard more voices, more footsteps, and then the siren starting up again.

All I could think of was Cooper sitting there on the john, his arms wrapped in towels, the brilliant red of his blood, the soft cool feel of his cheeks in my hands, the silky feel of his eyelids beneath my thumbs.

I felt the outline of his knife in the pocket of my pajama top, right over my heart. I was crying like a baby.

9

COOPER WOULD HAVE gagged.

They put him in a gray-cloth coffin and rolled it into the chapel on some kind of cart with wheels. One under-taker guy in front pulling, another behind pushing.

And who was right behind them, all done up in black with a white hankie, all sad and sniffly, some biker-gang guy walking beside her, holding her arm? Remembered she had a son after all.

Cooper's mother put a red rose on top of the casket. And if that wasn't enough, she bent down to kiss the lid.

The chapel was packed. Father Stewart was up at the front behind the altar. When the undertaker guys arrived he stretched out both arms, palms up, and we all got to our feet.

The Brothers were up at the front in rows of pews on both sides of the altar, and they were doing a funny kind of singing, sort of like chanting. All in Latin, so who knew what they were saying.

Once the coffin was up at the front and Cooper's mother and her biker boy sat down in the very first pew, Stewart turned both palms down and we all sat. Then the Brothers all stood up and did another hymn and when they were done, Stewart stood behind the altar, did a little chanting in Latin, then came around in front of the altar and looked directly at Cooper's mother.

"This is a very sad occasion, for you, Mrs. Cooper, and for us all," he said.

It was enough to make you choke. From where I was sitting, in the very back row, I couldn't see Cooper's mother in her funeral get-up. But I could see her plainly enough in my mind's eye, sprawled out on the floor of some dive, naked except for her panties, some loser flaked out on the floor nearby, beer bottles everywhere, Cooper and the social worker in the doorway. I could see Cooper's face as he took it all in.

"How can we begin to understand the nature of your sorrow and your loss," said Stewart.

Sweet Jesus. As Cooper would have said, just loud enough to be heard from the very back, *Spare us, please.*

Then Stewart got on a roll.

"We are gathered here this morning to mourn the passing of an exceptional young man. It is always difficult to lose one of our young people, but it is especially so in this case as Timothy chose his moment and method of leaving us. It is always a tragedy and something of a mystery when the young choose to end their lives."

What fucking mystery? Take a good look at that asshole to your right, Stewart. His name is Prince. And he killed Cooper.

"Timothy was an exceptionally sensitive and talented boy. Like many such boys, he was tormented by troubles which had touched his life long before he came to us. And though we did our best to help him deal with those troubles, sadly whatever we did was not enough. The demons he was dealing with finally got the better of him despite our best efforts to help him."

Jeezus fuck. I got up and edged my way down the pew and out the door and down the stairs and out into the yard. It took me two cigarettes and three trips around the yard to cool off.

Shit.

I went back inside and up to the dorm. Cooper's bed had been stripped, a new set of neatly folded sheets placed at the foot of the bare mattress, a folded blanket on top of them, the pillow on top of the blanket.

I didn't want to look at it, but I couldn't help myself. I patted the pillow on my way to the washroom.

Hey, Cooper.

They'd told Rozey to take down all the doors from the toilet stalls. As if that was going to change anything.

"Father Stewart told me to do it," said Rozey. "Oh, boy, Teddy, he was mad. He told me take down the doors before someone else... you know." Poor Rozey. He could hardly get the words out before his eyes welled up.

I went to the last stall and stood there for a minute, just staring at it. Then I sat where Cooper had been sitting, looked down at the floor where all his blood had been. I stayed there maybe two or three minutes. Then I went back out to the dorm and lay down on Cooper's old bed, curled up around his pillow until I heard the chapel bells. A couple of minutes later, I could hear voices echoing up through the halls and the stairwells. I went over to the windows facing the front yard and looked down at the hearse parked in the circle drive. The back door was open.

A few minutes later the undertaker guys came out with the coffin, slid it into the hearse and closed the door. Cooper's old lady and her boyfriend got into the car right behind the hearse and they took off.

Bye, Cooper.

———

I WENT TO my locker, pulled out Wordsworth, went over and sat on Cooper's bed. I'd grabbed the book the night Cooper killed himself. After we came back to the dorm, I reached inside his pillowcase, pulled it out and put it in my locker for safekeeping.

He'd written something on pretty well every page, and pretty well all of the writing had to do with Prince. What Prince was doing to him. What he was doing to Prince. He'd dated all the entries and after each one he ranted on about Prince.

Now and then there were things about Rozey and me, about our trips to the farm, fishing. But then it was back into the sewer of his life. I couldn't read more than a page without closing the book, coming up for air. I sat there flipping the pages, glancing at his handwriting, but it was more than I could stomach.

Cooper's funeral was Tuesday. The days after that just felt like a blur. The weird thing was, no one talked about Cooper. And after Stewart's pukey little sermon, the priests never mentioned his name again. It was like everyone just pretended he'd never been there.

Except for Bro Joe. One day after supper I was out in the yard, me and Wordsworth. I couldn't open it. But for some strange reason I had to have it with me. I carried it everywhere.

It was freezing. The sun was long gone and the first stars were winking away up there and the wind had come up, blowing the snow around. I was down by the fence line to the very back of the yard, looking up at Cooper's hill, watching the cars and trucks heading for the great beyond.

"Pretty, isn't it?"

Jeezus. Brother Joe. Where had he come from?

"I'm so sorry," he said.

"It's all right. I just didn't hear you coming."

"About your friend," said Brother Joe. "About Timothy."

"Thanks."

"It was a terrible thing," he said. "It must have been horrible for you to find him. I'm so sorry you had to experience that." He was looking right at me when he said it. Like he wanted to make sure I knew that he meant it.

"Thanks," I said.

"I'm sure it's still all too close for you," he said. "But if ever you feel like talking about what you're going through, I'd be pleased to listen." He smiled. His chapel smile.

"Thanks, Bro."

"I'm just going to take another turn around the yard. You're welcome to join me if you feel like company. But perhaps you'd prefer to be alone." That was one of the things I liked about Bro Joe. He was always careful not to corner you.

"Yeah," I said. "A little company wouldn't hurt."

We padded through the snow.

"Is it true, what they say?" I said. "That you sleep out here?"

"Yes," he said. "Not so much in the winter anymore. But in the good weather I quite regularly like to bed down beneath the trees."

"Why?"

"I love to look at the stars," he said. "Stars beyond stars. Galaxies beyond galaxies. We have no idea how vast the heavens really are except to say they are vast beyond our ability to understand such vastness. They give you a little glimpse of eternity, I think." He turned. "When you're confronted by such immensity, we all seem pretty small and insignificant."

"I always feel alone when I think of stuff like that," I said.

"You're never alone, Teddy. The presence of God is all around you."

"Always around you, maybe," I said. "God and I don't have much to do with each other."

He turned to look at me. He had such a sad look in his eyes. "You don't believe?"

"It's kind of hard to imagine God's been hanging around this place," I said. "If he's supposed to see the little sparrow fall, how come he couldn't see Cooper falling? If there really is a God, don't you think he would have shown up in the washroom, pulled the knife out of Cooper's hand?"

Brother Joe shook his head and sighed. Then he looked at me.

"I have to say, Teddy, sometimes I wonder the same thing." He shook his head again. "I really do."

"If there's a God, how come he would let Prince do what he did to Cooper? How do you figure that?"

"It's not God I blame for that," he said.

"Who do you blame?"

"I blame the bishop who sent him to us last summer. They said there was no proof of any wrongdoing. We should have done something. I should have done something. We'll all have to answer for that. Some of us are answering in our own way right now."

We had wound up back by the school, by the back door.

"You want to see proof, Bro?" I opened up Cooper's book. "Have a look."

As if Joe was going to do anything about it. But for some reason I just wanted to shove it right in his face.

He read for a moment, flipped the page. Closed the book.

"My God," he said. Handed it back. "Who knows you have this?"

"Nobody. Right now."

"What will you do with it?"

"Haven't decided." We stood there for another few minutes. "I guess I better be getting in, Bro."

———

SATURDAY WITHOUT COOPER was tough. Right after breakfast I went out into the yard and around the corner and looked at the spot where he and I always sat. I looked around for one of the butts he was always spiraling away, looking for any sign of him. I could only stand doing that for about two minutes.

Right after study hall I headed downtown. Rozey was parked on the side street in front of the school.

"Hey," he said, leaning across and opening the passenger door.

"Hey, Rozey." I got in, rubbed my hands in front of the heater vent. "Man, it's freezing out there."

"It's January," said Rozey.

"Yeah. I know. I can tell by all the snow."

He laughed.

"You know that road back of town, the one that we can see from the school? Goes up the hill?"

"The highway?"

"Yeah. Can we go up there? To the top of that hill?"

"Sure."

Ten minutes later we pulled to the side of the highway at the top of the hill overlooking the town.

"Mind if I just walk up the road a bit by myself?"

Rozey shut the engine. "Go ahead."

I got out and walked up the shoulder of the road, bare gravel where the snowplows had scraped by. From the crest of the hill I expected to be able to see forever, but all I could see was more hills humping up into the distance, hill after hill after hill.

I turned and looked back the other way, toward the school. I could see the building and the playing fields, the back door where we came out after breakfast, the area around the corner where Cooper and I always sat looking up at the place where I was now standing.

I imagined Cooper and me standing right at this spot, our thumbs out, waiting for a long-haul trucker to come and haul us all the way to the west coast.

So much for that.

I headed back to Rozey's truck.

"See what you wanted?"

"Yeah."

Rozey pulled a U-turn in the middle of the highway and we headed back into town.

"How about a few hands of cribbage?"

"Yeah," I said. We drove through town and out to his place, trudged through the snow to the house.

Rozey tossed a couple more logs into the woodstove and we sat there playing cards and drinking pop. We'd been there maybe fifteen, twenty minutes when I looked across the table at Rozey. He was looking down at his cards, waiting for me to make a move. Then he looked up.

Wouldn't you know it, as soon as he did that I started crying.

"I still can't believe it," I said. "That poor little bastard." Wiped my nose on my sleeve.

"I miss him, too," said Rozey. "You and him were my pals."

"You know what bothers me the most?" I said. "I should have known he would do something like that. When I look back now it's so obvious I can't believe it." I looked up at Rozey. "You know what Cooper said once? He told me nobody ever loved him."

"He was wrong," said Rozey. "You were his best friend."

I looked at him.

"I'm so pissed that he would do this." I jammed my cigarette butt into the ashtray. "I'm just so pissed."

All of a sudden I was crying again. Rozey just sat there and let me go at it. After a while I stopped crying, sat there sniffling like a little kid.

"Feel like some cookies?"

"Would you mind taking me back, Rozey? I think I just feel like being by myself."

"Cookies for the road?" He held up the jar.

"Sure. Sounds great."

Rozey didn't say anything until he pulled into the drive at St. Iggy's, drove right up to the front door.

I looked over at him, a little surprised.

"They said I should never be with the boys," he said. "But you're my pal. I'm drivin' you to the door is all."

I smiled. "Thanks, Rozey."

I got out and went up to the front doors, turned and waved at Rozey, then went in and up the stairs.

"Teddy?"

Jeezus. "Dr. Harrison? What are you doing here?"

"Waiting to see you, actually. Would you mind?" He motioned toward the door of the waiting room right across from Stewart's office.

I stopped just inside the door.

Dr. Harrison looked at my nose. "Just as I predicted, now you do look like a prize fighter." Did, too. There was a lump in the middle of my nose, and it was a little crooked.

"The girls are going to love it," he said. "Everything else all right?"

"Yeah."

A big guy was sitting on the sofa. A really big guy. He stood up, took a couple of steps toward me. Must have been six-five anyway. Two-sixty, two-seventy.

"I'm Dan Evans." He stuck out a hand. It was the size of both of mine.

I shook his hand, turned to look at Dr. Harrison.

"Mr. Evans is investigating matters here at St. Iggy's," Dr. Harrison said.

"What matters?"

He shut the door, motioned for me to take a chair. "I talked to Mr. Evans right after your encounter with Father Sullivan. He's been looking into that and now, of course, he's been investigating Timothy Cooper's death."

"I'm sorry about your friend," said Evans. "About Timothy."

"Thanks."

"You were the one who found him?"

I nodded.

Evans sat up on the edge of the sofa, opened a little notebook, put it on his knee.

"Can you tell me about that? About finding him?"

I told them the whole story. How I went into the washroom, saw the blood on the floor.

Evans was writing it all down. Then he looked up.

"Did he say anything to you, once you got into the stall?"

"I told him I wanted to go get help. He said he would hate me forever if I did."

"Anything else?"

My eyes were welling up. I shook my head. Shook it again.

"What did you do then?"

"I went and told Prince."

"Why Prince?"

"Because I wanted that sonofabitch to see what he'd done."

There was silence in the room. Evans looked at Dr. Harrison. Dr. Harrison looked at me.

"What he'd done?" he said.

"To Cooper. What happened to Cooper because of what he'd done."

"Tell me about that," said Evans.

I laid it all out. I went right back to the start of school, told them how Prince showed up to supervise showers, how he was always looking at us, how he started calling out boys after he shut the lights.

"Which boys?"

"I heard he called out a couple of guys in the senior dorm. But then he came over to our dorm and started on Cooper and it was pretty much Cooper all the time after that."

"Pretty much?" said Evans.

"And me. A couple of times."

He wanted the lowdown on that. I told him about the candles, the pictures in the drawer, the drink he gave me that made me feel so sick. He wanted to know what Prince had talked about and I told him.

"Did he molest you?" said Evans.

I looked at Dr. Harrison, then back at Evans.

"Put his . . . he put his hand on my . . . crotch."

"Did Timothy ever tell you what Prince was doing to him?"

"Sort of," I said.

"Sort of?"

I told him about the talk Cooper and I had. About him hating what Prince was doing to him, how it was all he could think about, how he thought maybe he did like it, like Prince was saying, that maybe he was turning into a homo because of it.

"Nothing more specific?"

I shook my head.

Evans finished writing, then looked up. "Did Cooper leave a note? Explaining things?"

"No," I said.

"Brother Joseph tells me you've got a book of Cooper's with some very telling remarks written in the margins. A book of poems by Wordsworth. I'd like to see it."

Holy shit. I couldn't believe it. Who would have guessed it would be Joe who'd go to the cops?

"Could you bring it down?"

Ten minutes later he was flipping through Wordsworth, turning it this way and that to read what Cooper had written in the margins. He spent quite a while doing that. Then he looked at me.

"You've read this?"

I nodded.

"Who else has read it?"

"Brother Joe. I showed it to him."

"Anyone else?"

I shook my head.

"I'm going to have to take this with me."

"Will I get it back?"

"I don't know. If you do, it won't be for a while." He stood up. "Thank you, Teddy. You've been a great help." Evans stopped by the door. "That night, in the bathroom, did you find a knife?"

I shook my head. There was no way he was getting the knife.

"No," I said.

He nodded. "Thanks. You've been very helpful."

"What are you going to do about Prince?"

"We're looking into it," he said.

I watched them leave.

Way to go, Joe. I still couldn't believe he'd actually gone to the cops. And I couldn't wait to see what was going to happen next.

———

I WAS LATE for mail call. Docherty was just finishing up with the letters. Then he started tossing the parcels.

"Oh, this one is heavy. Bet there are cookies in this one. Mr. Clemson." I raised my hand. He tossed it toward me. No one put up their hands to deflect it. I caught it with both hands. "Nice catch, Mr. Clemson. You ought to try out for the football team." Ha-ha.

I took my parcel up to the locker room, sat on the wooden bench in front of my locker and ripped off the paper. Mom had sent me a tin of my favorite peanut butter cookies, a carton of Export plains, some mints and gum, a couple of hot rod magazines and some new socks.

I opened her letter.

Dear Teddy,

Things are fine here at home. How are things there? I hope you're doing well with your studies. It seems so strange not to have you here. I wake up some mornings and find myself heading to your room to get you up for school and then remember that you're not here. I do miss having you around – even when you were being grumpy and unreasonable. I'm sure when you're back here with us, things will be much better for all of us.

Please don't think too badly of Henry. He really does have your best interests at heart. He can seem a bit tough, but he's really a very thoughtful and gentle man. I know you two didn't get off to a very good start but, honestly, I think a lot of that had to do with you being so angry at your father and at me. Breaking up is so hard on everyone. I'm sure you don't understand why this had to happen. But there was no way we could carry on. It really was for the best that he left. Have you heard from him? I'm enclosing his address if you haven't heard from him and want to write. I know he'd like to hear from you.

I'll sign off for now. I'm enclosing some spending money to get you through the next month or so.

Love,
Mom

She'd shoved some fives and tens into an envelope along with a slip of paper with my father's address. I put the money and her letter in the envelope and put it in my locker beneath my pile of underwear. I crumpled up the piece of paper with my father's address and tossed it in the garbage. I shoved the box into the bottom of my locker, closed the door and snapped the lock.

I know he'd like to hear from you.

Yeah. Right.

I headed for the door. But then, for some reason, I went back and got the ball of paper out of the garbage. Smoothed it out. Folded it up. Put it in my pocket.

———

SUPPER TIME, SMOKE time, shower time.

Brother Wilbur stood in the shower doorway.

"Where's Prince?" said Klemski.

"Father Prince is no longer with us," said Wilbur. "Let's go, gentlemen. Showers and bed."

Holy shit.

Lying in bed I couldn't get to sleep. My mind was buzzing. I pictured Dan Evans showing up at Prince's door, showing him Cooper's book. I could see the look on his face, totally stunned. I could see Evans handcuffing him and taking him down the stairs, shoving him in the back of the cop car.

I wondered what would happen next. If there was going to be a big trial. If I would have to testify. I started to think about exactly what I'd tell the judge.

Cooper would be so happy if he knew.

And if he hadn't made all those notes in the margin, there would have been no proof.

It was too good.

10

I woke up in a panic, all sweaty, heart racing, and it took me a few seconds to realize I'd been dreaming.

I'd been in Prince's room, all the candles going. We were on the couch, Prince at one end, me at the other.

He moved down and put his hand on my crotch. I wanted to move his hand, but I couldn't get my arms to work. It was like they were paralyzed.

He started rubbing me.

I jumped up from the couch. He grabbed my pajama top and tried to pull me toward him. I pulled back so hard the buttons popped off. He pulled the top off me. Left fingernail tracks right across my chest.

I was backing toward the door.

Then I reached down to get Cooper's switchblade out of my sock.

All of a sudden Prince had me by the wrist, twisted one arm behind my back, pulled my bottoms down around my knees and put his other hand around my cock.

Somehow I got Cooper's knife out, flipped the blade.

Then somehow Rozey was right behind me. He had a big Jeezus wrench in his hand. But when I turned, Prince grabbed the knife, pulled me toward him, put his arm around my neck.

Rozey went for Prince's wrist and twisted, hard. Prince yelled in pain and let me go. I scrambled away and then Rozey had a clear shot at him. He swung his wrench and caught Prince on the left shoulder. But just as Prince was reeling away, he lunged out with the knife, and suddenly Rozey was down on his knees, both hands holding his belly.

I started screaming.

And that's when I woke up.

―――――

But that's not the way things ended.

The morning after Prince left, we got up, made our beds, got dressed, went to chapel, went to breakfast. The cafeteria was buzzing. Everyone knew Prince was gone. No one knew where. In geography class it was all Dunlop could do to get the whispering to stop. He was rattling on about the Canadian Shield, had to keep interrupting himself to tell us to pay attention, when there was a knock at the door. He went over and opened it, stepped out in the hall, came back in.

"Mr. Clemson."

"Yeah?"

"Yes, Father?"

"Yes, Father."

"Come here."

I got up, started for the door.

"Bring your books."

My books? I gathered up my stuff. Klemski gave me his what-the-hell look. I shrugged, headed for the door.

Stewart was standing there.

"Come with me." We walked down the hall to his office. "Have a chair, Mr. Clemson."

I sat in one of the chairs facing his desk. It was the first time I'd been in his office since Day One at St. Iggy's. Creepy as ever. Same dim light. Same musty smell. Same bleeding Jesus on the wall.

Stewart took out his strap, laid it on the desk, sat down, leaned back just as he'd done that first day, did the same little prayer thing with his fingers against his lips. Just sat there for a minute without saying anything. Giving me The Eye.

I couldn't stand it any longer.

"What's up?"

Stewart sat up, put his elbows on the desk.

"I'm expelling you, Mr. Clemson."

"What?"

"Your father is coming to get you. He will be here this afternoon. I want you to go upstairs and pack your things and bring them to the waiting room across the hall. You will remain there until your father arrives."

"Why are you doing this?"

"You are a disruptive force, Mr. Clemson. You are, as your teacher Mr. Little warned us, a troublesome boy. You are willful and rude and coarse and vulgar. You have been uncooperative and difficult since the day you arrived. Despite our best efforts to bring you into line you continue to cause trouble. We can no longer tolerate your behavior."

"It's about Prince, isn't it?"

He glared at me.

"It's about what I said to that detective, isn't it? And you know what? Now that the cops have Cooper's book, they're going to nail his ass. And yours, too, probably."

You know how sometimes when people smile at you in a certain way, your stomach does a little flip? That's the kind of smile Stewart had on his face.

He leaned back, opened the drawer of his desk, pulled out Cooper's book.

"This book?"

"That's mine."

"This is not your property, Mr. Clemson. In fact, I could have you arrested for theft."

"The cop gave it to you?"

Stewart shook his head. "Mr. Evans works for us, Mr. Clemson. The Diocese. He fixes things for us. Like this."

He held up the book, then put it back in the drawer, shut the drawer, leaned forward and put his elbows back on his desk.

"You're not quite as smart as you thought, are you, Mr. Clemson?"

"What happened to Prince?"

"Go pack your things, Mr. Clemson."

Took me all of five minutes to jam everything into my duffel bag. I came back downstairs, tossed it into the waiting room and headed for the door. I was about halfway down the drive when I heard Stewart.

"Mr. Clemson, get back here."

I didn't slow down. Didn't turn around. Just held up my left hand. Gave him the finger. Kept on going. I was so fucking mad I could hardly see. I was shaking like crazy.

I could have killed Stewart. And I especially could have killed Brother Joe.

Jeezus.

I went up one side of Main Street and down the other. It was freezing, but I was walking so fast I was sweating. The shaking had stopped, but I was still so angry I could hardly think straight.

Up the street and back again.

And then I was passing by the hardware and who should be there, standing behind the counter, looking out the window directly at me?

Lucy gave me a little wave. I waved back.

Then she smiled.

That smile.

———

I OPENED UP my duffel bag, shoved through all the clothes to get to my notebook at the bottom of the bag. I took a pencil and my art book and headed for the stairs to the basement.

"Hey, Teddy." Rozey looked up at the clock. "Shouldn't you be in class?"

I pulled up a box and sat down. "You're not going to believe this."

He didn't. He sat there, didn't move all through my story, then just shook his head.

"Jeez." He shook his head again. "Oh, boy, Teddy. I'm going to miss you."

"I'm going to miss you, too."

What else was there to say?

I opened my notebook, flipped through until I found the sketch I'd done of Lucy. The one I couldn't finish.

"Give me a minute, Rozey."

"What are you doing?"

"You'll see."

Didn't take me ten minutes. I ripped the page from the notebook and handed it to Rozey. His eyes went all red and watery.

"That's the most beautiful picture I've ever seen. Thanks, Teddy. Thanks a million." He took another look at the drawing. "And I know right where I'm going to put it. I'm going to put it in a frame and hang it in the bedroom. Across from my bed. That way I can say goodnight to Lucy every night and good morning every morning. Just like we really did get married."

He looked down at the picture, then up at me. Then his chin got all wrinkly. He stood up and gave me a hug.

"Bye, Teddy."

"Bye, Rozey. Good luck with the boat."

"Thanks."

"Think of me when you finally get out to the ocean."

He started to say something. Then he just shook his head.

———

I FOUND JOE just where I thought I'd find him, out in the yard back by the fence. When he saw me coming, he looked scared.

"Teddy, I'm sorry."

"How could you do it, Joe?"

"I was bound," he said.

"Bound?"

"By my oath," he said.

"What oath?"

"My oath of obedience."

"Obedience?"

"My first duty is to God. My second duty is to my bishops and superiors. I had to tell them. It was my duty."

"Duty? Shit, Joe. What about Cooper? What about me? What about all the kids Prince is going to fuck wherever they send him? What about your duty to the next kid who's going to kill himself because of that pervert? Do you think your God is going to like that?"

"I'm sorry, Teddy."

"Really?" I shook my head. "I thought you were my friend, Joe. But you know what? Day One, Cooper said you can't trust anyone in a place like this. How right was that?" I turned and walked away.

"Teddy?"

I just kept on walking. Back into the school, into the waiting room, grabbed my bag and went out the door, walked down the drive, put my bag down, put my toque on, wrapped my scarf around my neck twice, sat down on my bag.

I was on my seventh cigarette and just about frozen solid when my dad pulled up in his Ford. He got out, came up to me.

"Hi, Teddy."

Same dad. Same black wavy hair, just like mine. Same blue eyes, just like mine.

He held out his hand.

I'd never shaken hands with him in my life. I looked up at him, then shook his hand.

Same dimpled smile, just like mine.

"What are you doing out here?"

"I couldn't stand being in that fucking place for one more minute."

"Let's get you in the car. You must be frozen." He opened the trunk, tossed my bag in, slammed the trunk.

I got in the car, held my hands up near the heater vents, tried to rub some feeling back into them. My dad put the car in gear, started to pull away.

I took a last look at St. Iggy's, looked up at the dorm windows on the third floor, imagined Cooper waving at me, pathetic little fingers all gnawed to ratshit. Jeezus.

Then I started to think about Klemski and the other guys and how weird it was going to be to never see them again. I sure as hell wouldn't miss St. Iggy's, but I'd miss those guys. Anderson and Henderson and Zits and Hatfield with all his nutty jokes. And Rita and Freddy. And Rozey, for sure.

My eyes were welling up. I wiped them with my palms.

"You okay?"

"Yeah."

We drove through town, past Rita's diner and out to the highway. We went up the hill, past the spot that Cooper and I were always looking at, the spot right near the top. Then we went over the hill and over the next and just kept going.

My dad didn't say two words all the way.

I got thinking about what Hemingway had said, about a man being destroyed but not defeated. And I thought maybe he was wrong, that sometimes you could be defeated and then destroyed. Like Cooper. And that got me thinking about Cooper for a while and that got me thinking about what Rozey had said about broken hearts. I thought maybe he was right.

Maybe it would just take time.

We were on the road another half hour, maybe more. Not a word. My dad was looking at the road, I was looking at the rocks and trees. Too weird. He had the radio going, cranked right up.

Finally he shut it off.

"I'm sorry," he said.

I turned to look at him.

"For everything," he said. "I'm embarrassed and I'm ashamed. I'm only hoping you'll give me a second chance."

What do you say to that? I had no clue. I just looked straight ahead. We covered another mile or two.

Finally I turned to face him.

"I guess."

He reached over and grabbed the back of my neck, gave it a little squeeze.

"Thanks," he said.

Another few miles and he said, "I don't know what went on in that place. But when you feel like it, I'd like you to tell me about it."

I nodded. "Okay." Another six or seven miles. "So, where are we going?"

"I got a little cottage down by the bay."

"You and who else?"

"Just me."

"What about what's-her-name?"

"She's gone," he said.

Another mile or so. "So, it'll just be you and me?"

"Yup."

I spent the next half hour or so thinking about that, thinking about what it would be like living with my dad, just the two of us, in that cottage down on the bay.

I could imagine waking up in the morning and going down on the beach to see the clouds and the birds, the boats out on the water. Sitting out there on a log in the evening, watching the sun go down over the hills on the far side of the bay.

Seemed like it might be sort of like Cooper's beach.

I thought maybe that would be all right.

"Sounds okay," I said.

"What sounds okay?"

"The cottage," I said.

"Good."

Author's Thanks

THANK YOU TO Margaret Atwood and Graeme Gibson, Joan Barfoot, Mary Deck and Martin Deck, Jacquie Gibson and Phil Gibson, Mary Anne Mulhern, Gemma Smyth and Adam Vasey, Kirsten Vasey and Mark Odrcich and, especially, to Marilyn Vasey. Some read the manuscript in its various versions and offered a host of thoughtful comments and suggestions for improvements. Others offered encouragement and advice. I'm indebted to all.

Thanks also to Doug Hewitt, librarian for the Essex County Law Association, and attorneys Frank Montello, Carl Cohen, Ruth Stewart and Ted Perfect for their help with legal history.

And a special thank-you to editor Shelley Tanaka who saw not only what was on the page and needed improvement but what was not yet on the page and needed to be.

About the Author

PAUL VASEY HAS had a stellar career as a print, radio and TV journalist (*Windsor Star*, *Hamilton Spectator* and as the CBC morning host in Windsor and Victoria), and has been awarded a Southam Fellowship for Journalists. A boarding-school survivor, he is the author of five novels for adults, as well as *Kids in the Jail: Why Our Young Offenders Do the Things They Do*. He also sits on the board of Maryvale, a mental-health treatment center for children and adolescents.

Paul lives in Windsor with his wife, Marilyn.